Let's Go Gardening!

A Young Person's Guide to the Garden

The Lutterworth Press
Cambridge

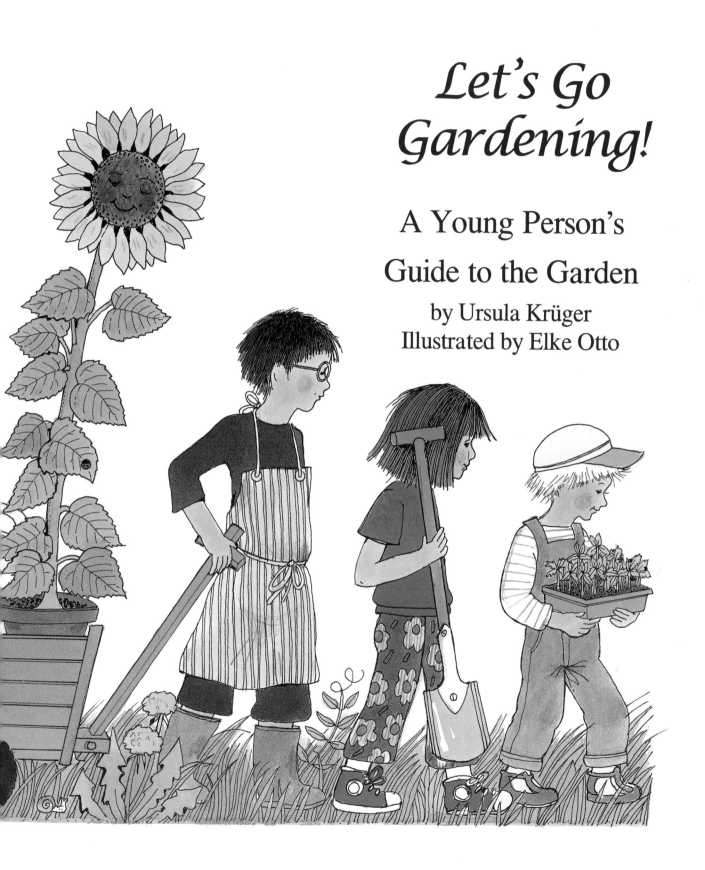

Let's Go Gardening!

A Young Person's
Guide to the Garden

by Ursula Krüger
Illustrated by Elke Otto

Contents

Foreword

Do you know what plants are? Of course you do! Roses are plants, trees are too, grass is a plant, and so are flowers. They can grow out in the countryside, in gardens, on balconies, or indoors in pots on the windowsill.

It's a lot of fun to grow your own plants, whether in your parents' garden or indoors. You just won't believe it! Poke a bean into some damp earth and after a few days a tiny leaf appears. Soon there are more, and if you water it a bit the stalk gets longer and longer, and after only a few weeks a little bean has turned into a huge plant with lots of new beans hanging from its pods. It's just like magic! All you need is earth, a bean (that's the seed), water, light and warmth. If you want to become a gardener you will need to know a few rules, but it's all really quite easy. After you have read this book, you'll be all set to compete with professional gardeners (well, almost).

Wishing you lots of fun and much success.

Ursula Krüger

What is Earth?

The gardener has thousands of helpers. You can't see most of them because they are too small, and many of them live in the earth and don't let us see them very much. But there is one that you have almost certainly seen in damp grass: the earthworm.

It knows a great deal about earth, how it is made and what is in it, because the worm is one of those creatures that produces earth. Its story is really interesting, but let's get the worm to tell us itself.

"My name is Wiggle and I'm a worm. Now I would be extremely grateful if you would NOT say 'yuk!' or anything like that! I get quite upset when that happens, you know, and when I'm upset terrible things happen to my stomach. And my stomach is important not just for me but for you as well. I'll tell you why a bit later.

"First a few words about me and my relations. There are lots of us and we are everywhere, all across the world. As for me, I'm an ordinary earthworm and live in fields, meadows and your garden. Sometimes I meet my uncle there, who is a dew worm. He's much bigger than me, 30 cm long and amazingly strong. Just imagine, he tunnels as far as 3 metres into the ground! I won't ever get bigger than 20 cm and my tunnels aren't so deep. Our tunnels are important because they loosen up the earth. My cousin also contributes to your garden. She's a muckworm, doesn't get bigger than 14 cm, and is also called the Tennessee Wiggler or the Red Californian. Her tunnels are only about 20 cm deep but she makes great humus out of the compost.

"Now, about my stomach. I just adore rotting leaves and other fallen-off bits of plants. I wriggle up one of my tunnels - usually at night - and pick up a nice bit of mouldy leaf from the surface. I take it back down into my tunnel and the feast begins. To me it tastes just as good as spaghetti with tomato sauce might taste to you. I don't like fresh things as much - they have to be a bit mouldy.

"My little friends the microbes, or micro-organisms, help to provide me with dinners with just the right amount of mould. They are so tiny that you need a microscope (that's like a magnifying glass) to see them.

"Some people have accused me of eating the roots of plants. Now this is nonsense, because I don't have any teeth and so I can't bite. I have to just suck in my food straight into my stomach. And as for my other end . . . now how can I say it?

What comes out of there is what you call worm humus, or castings. It's really concentrated earth, top quality. And that's why I'm so important. My long intestines separate out the individual parts of the dead plant material, so in my humus you find, for example, nitrogen, phosphorous, potassium, calcium and magnesium. These things are plant food, and the new plants need them to grow just as you need milk, bread, fat, fruit, meat, vegetables and other things like that."

This is Wiggle stretched out.

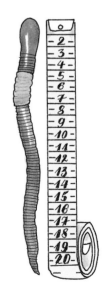

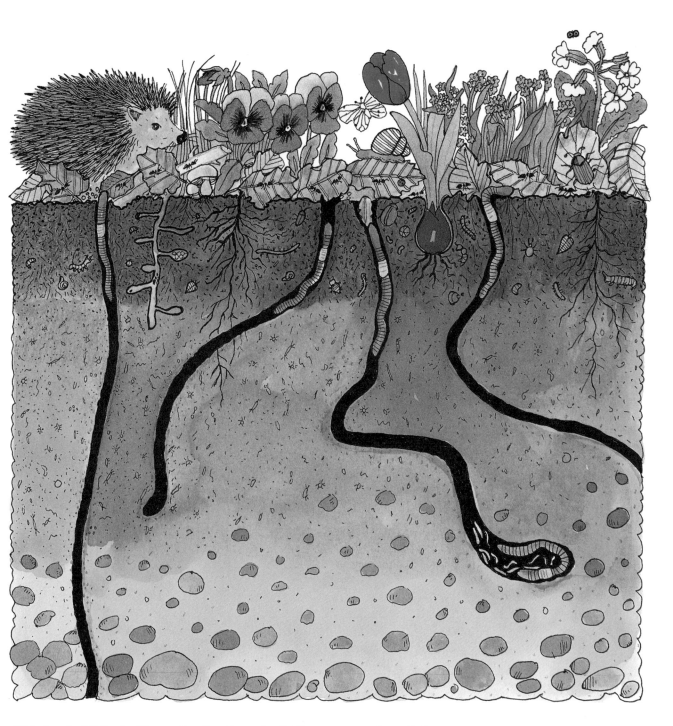

This is what it looks like under the flowerbed. You can see where I dig my tunnels and where we worms, together with many other animals, spend most of our life.

But I'm not the only one to produce humus. The earth is just teeming with organisms which all have their own task. Imagine it's like a big factory. The raw materials are in the soil, and they include waste plant material, dead animals, and living animals that are eaten by other animals. They may be pulled apart, ground up, dissolved or eaten whole. The workers in this factory are the billions of organisms living in the soil. These include ants, beetles, spiders, centipedes, snails, insect larvae and the tiny micro-organisms I mentioned before. 'Micro' comes from the Greek language and means 'small'. 'Organism' means 'living thing'. Organisms include bacteria, fungus, algae and yeast. Since the world began we have all been helping to keep up the supply of earth by eating natural waste products and also each other.

Just imagine what would happen if all the leaves from the trees, all the wilted flowers and grass, and dead roots and animals just lay there. The world would look like a rubbish heap.

I hope you're not put off by this! These processes are not revolting, but natural. The fertile soil continuously produced by me and the other workers provides the basis for every living thing: all plants, animals and people. It's a big circle: the plants grow in the earth. They need the nutrients I

Just as children like different sorts of cake, so different plants like different sorts of soil.

produce with my friends from plant waste in order to grow.

Many animals eat the plants which grow in the earth - you do too. So if I didn't produce worm humus, then no plants could grow, animals would have nothing to eat, and there would be no more apples, carrots, fried chicken or anything else for you either.

Do you understand now how important my stomach is for you?

And how essential it is that I always get enough old leaves and wilted flowers to eat? Well then, I'd be grateful if you left a few

lying around for me. Proper gardeners say: what grows in the garden should stay in the garden - except of course for the fruit and vegetables that you need for your meals.

Now it doesn't look very nice if there are dead leaves and plants lying everywhere. That's why people collect them in one corner of the garden, in the compost heap. That's where my cousin the compost worm lives.

He is busy eating and digesting everything. He produces the best soil you can imagine.

A large garden might have several compost heaps, but a small garden will only need one.

Not all soil is the same. You have probably noticed that soil has various colours. Some is light brown, some dark brown, some reddish. And it feels different. Soil doesn't just consist of worm humus. It contains minerals as well. These are stones that have become powder. Animals don't change stones into powder, the weather does. Wind, water, frost and heat wear away the stone.

You have probably held a pebble in your hand. It was not always like that: it was loosened from a rock face by frost, then it fell into a stream where, over millions of years, the water made it smooth. What rubbed off the stone sank into the ground. And so the colour of the stones that have been lying around influences the colour of the earth.

The colour is also influenced by other things. Very dark earth contains many nutrients and shows that I've been busy. You can imagine it to be like cake. One sort of cake may contain lots of sultanas, another sort may contain lots of nuts. Some contain lots of fat, others don't. There are cakes made with yeast, there are sponges, gingerbreads and biscuits. You might prefer one sort and your friend another.

Plants are just the same. Some like sandy soil, others like gravel, some like dampness and others like dryness.

Nature's cycle works like this: you eat a carrot and throw the top onto the compost heap. The worm eats the carrot top and produces worm humus, which provides food for a new carrot to grow.

You're sure to want to know what sort of soil you have in your garden. A scientist can work it out exactly with complicated equipment. You can work it out roughly all by yourself.

Do the hand test. It goes like this: Take two handfuls of soil and see whether it runs through your fingers, like sand at the beach. If it does, then the soil contains a lot of sand, which consists of tiny pieces of stone. But if you can squeeze the soil into a ball or other shapes, then it is a clay soil. If the ball doesn't really stick together, then the soil contains a

The water test, which helps to show the quality of the earth and whether it is mainly made of sand or clay.

You can learn about the type and quality of soil by doing the hand test. (Have a look at the photos on the opposite page)

lot of humus and is very good. We worms have been busy there!

There is also the jar of water test. Ask your parents for a large glass jar and put about five centimetres of soil in it (don't take it from the surface - dig down about 20 centimetres to collect your sample). Then pour in water to about five centimetres below the top of the jar and stir it. Now you have to wait.

After a while the soil will sink to the bottom of the jar, since it is heavier than water. If everything sinks to the bottom and the water above remains almost clear, then the soil contains a lot of sand. If not so much soil sinks and the water is muddy, then the soil contains clay.

If there are crumbs of soil floating about on top, the water is brownish but clear, and the rest of the soil has sunk to the bottom, then the soil contains lots of good things that plants like.

It is also important to know whether soil is acid or alkaline. You can find that out yourself too. Chemists and garden shops sell testing paper or kits. It is probably best to ask your parents to help you with this.

You can of course buy soil from shops. There is soil specially mixed for plants in window boxes and pots, called potting compost. You need to tell the shop assistant what sort of plants you want the potting compost for.

You can buy different types of soil: standard potting compost suitable for most plants (top left), cactus mix (top right) and seed raising mix for growing baby plants (below).

The soil in the top photo is sandy and runs through your fingers. Soil containing lots of clay can easily be squeezed into a ball as in the middle photo. The dark soil in the last photo is especially good as it contains lots of humus.

11

Gardening Equipment

So, now you know what soil is and how it is made. Wiggle the Worm has wriggled back into the ground. By the way, about 200 earthworms can live in one cubic metre of earth - if they can find enough to eat.

Before you begin to garden, you must have the right equipment. It is important that children's equipment is not too heavy and has a handle of the right length. Some garden centres have children's equipment as well as adults' equipment. You should be there when your equipment is being bought so that you can try it out. Pretend you're digging in the garden or raking something. You will notice immediately if the handle is too long or if a hoe is too heavy. You can buy a shovel, spade, rake, hoe and leaf rake as attachments in a set together with a handle. You attach whatever you need to the handle when you want to use it. Very young children can practise with the sandpit spade.

Balcony gardeners and pot plant gardeners have an easier time finding equipment. There are special small spades and hoes which you can also use in the garden.

You can borrow some equipment from your parents: hand trowels, the dibble for planting, a string to be tied between two sticks for marking rows for sowing seeds. If you are old enough, you can use secateurs when wilted leaves need to be removed, or chives cut for a salad, or flowers picked for your parents. But ask someone to explain to you exactly how they work, and be careful!

Other practical things to have are small plastic buckets, a children's wheelbarrow or a cart that can be pulled along when you need to move things around. And you will need a small watering can with a sprinkler head.

Although it might seem a nuisance at the time, you should always clean your tools after using them and put them back in the tool shed, or wherever you're supposed to keep them, otherwise your parents may be annoyed. It's also much easier to work with clean equipment that can always be found when it's needed.

The right equipment will make your work in the garden easier. Have a look around a garden centre with your parents - perhaps you could ask for garden tools for your birthday.

Seeds

Whether you have a small plot in your parents' garden, a window box on the balcony, or a pot on the windowsill, everything starts with a seed. What's a seed? you ask. And where do seeds come from? Sunny the sunflower seed will explain it to you.

"Yes, I'm a seed. Seeds come in many forms: apple pips, plum stones, grain, and seeds as fine as dust or sand.

"Beans and peas are also seeds, so too are cucumber seeds and the small pips you find in grapes.

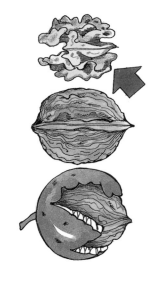

The walnut seed is delicious so it is well protected both by its hard inner shell and outer soft skin.

Try to count all the seeds in a sunflower. They make a tasty snack for birds.

We usually eat all a tomato's seeds when we eat one.

Rose seeds are to be found in the fruit of the rose, the rosehip.

Hazelnut seeds, like walnuts, are protected by a hard shell.

14

"Some seeds, such as cherry stones, are to be found inside fruit. The cherry stone's hard shell is just a covering. The actual seed is inside, and is soft and looks like a nut. It's the same with walnuts. They have a fleshy, green skin, but then comes the hard shell that you have to crack if you want to get at the tasty nut inside, the seed.

But remember that not all seeds are edible, and some are actually poisonous to humans."

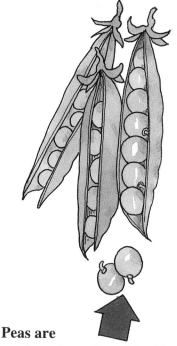

Peas are seeds and are found inside soft pods.

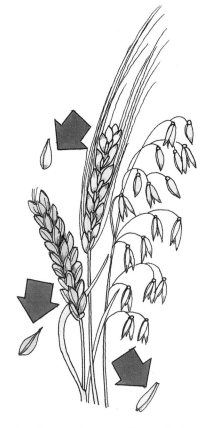

Grain, such as wheat (left), barley (centre) and oats (right), is especially important for us, because we make flour from its seed, and flour is used to bake bread and cakes.

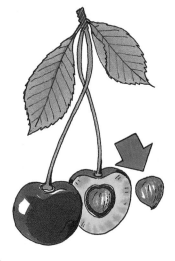

We eat only the fruit of cherry and spit out the stone, which contains the seed.

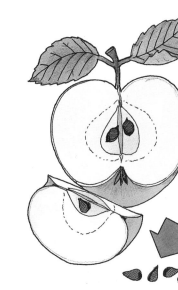

Apple seeds are hidden in the core.

"I'm sure you would like to know how I'm formed. It's like this: plants have flowers. Apple trees do, so do roses and violets, and I do too. Each flower contains both male and female parts, like a married couple, which is made up of a man and a woman. The male parts are the stamens (there are always a lot of these) and the female part is the pistil (there is only one of these). There is pollen at the top end of the stamens, which is usually yellow but sometimes red. The top end of the pistil, known as the stigma, is sticky. The base of the pistil contains the ovary. And then something happens that you've often seen: bees, bumble-bees and butterflies fly from one flower to another. They are looking for nectar, the sweet juice contained within the flowers. Insects like nectar very much. When they collect nectar from a flower, pollen sticks to their bodies. They then fly to the next flower, taking the pollen with them. The sticky stigma of the next flower picks up some of this pollen. If the pollen matches the stigma - rose pollen for a rose stigma, tomato pollen for a tomato stigma - then the pollen travels down the inside of the pistil to the ovary and fertilises it.

"If this all happens to a sunflower I begin to grow. Or a tomato grows, or a pear. Sometimes only one seed is formed, as with a peach, and sometimes many seeds are formed, as in my family, sunflowers."

A butterfly drinking nectar from a buddleia. In doing this it will pick up and transport pollen at the same time.

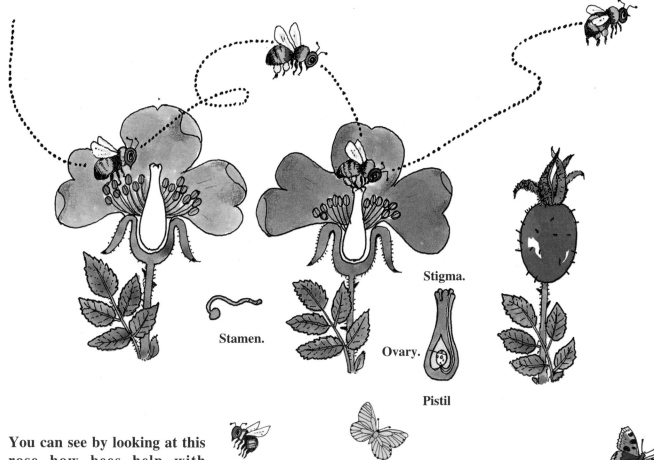

Stamen.

Stigma.

Ovary.

Pistil

You can see by looking at this rose how bees help with fertilization. The bee lands on the first rose to collect nectar. At the same time it brushes against the stamens and collects pollen on its legs, like a pair of yellow trousers. The bee flies to the next flower, taking the pollen with it. A few grains of pollen from the first flower stick to the stigma of the next flower and fertilise the egg. Eventually a lovely fat rosehip develops, containing many seeds.

"Sometimes the wind transports pollen on to the stigma. If neither the wind nor the insects get pollen to the right place then you will have to help. This might be necessary if the plant is indoors or if there aren't enough insects in the garden because an unwise adult has scared them away with poisonous sprays. You will need a fine brush. Gently brush over the stamens and then over the stigma, and that's all it takes. This process is often carried out in nursery glasshouses too.

"Seeds are all miniature miracles of nature. We all contain the beginnings of a new plant. Apple seeds can grow into apple trees, rosehips into roses, pumpkin seeds into pumpkins. You don't believe me? What I've told you here is all quite true. Believe me, and try it out. You might not be able to see the new plant inside me, but if you plant me in some soil and take care of me properly, then you'll see for yourself just what one small seed can do. Bye for now! I'll see you in a few pages."

Inside

You can become a gardener even if your parents don't have a garden. You can make a mini garden on a balcony, if it's strong enough, or on windowsills. Ask if you might have your own tub on the balcony. If you are a bit bigger you might ask for a box to hang over the railing, but this isn't a good idea for smaller gardeners. A box like that might be too high for you, and that would be dangerous for you to work at.

A tub on the floor of the balcony, or on a stand (such as a box or a small table) would be better. Put it at a height that you find comfortable to work at. Older children might find this a good idea too.

Even a windowsill is big enough for some plants. It's up to you whether you plant things in a tub or in individual pots. It depends a bit on the plants, too. A tomato plant needs a pot all to itself, but you can sow several radishes in one container. Busy Lizzies prefer to be alone, but cacti and succulents, those funny-looking plants with fleshy leaves, are happy to share.

There are round pots and square ones, tall ones and shallow ones. Window boxes can be as long as the whole window sill or much shorter. Some are made of plastic and are very light, others are made of clay and are very heavy. Use plastic pots and boxes, because plants and water (remember, you'll have to water your mini garden) are quite heavy. If the container is heavy when it's empty, then you might not be able to move it at all once it's full!

Whether your garden is on the windowsill or the balcony it's important to place a saucer under the pot. Water will run out the bottom of the pot through the drainage holes when you water the plant. The drainage holes are there so that the plant doesn't 'drown'. If you don't use a saucer then water might run along the windowsill, down the wallpaper and on to the carpet . . . and you might run into trouble!

You have decisions to make. You can buy plants in flower shops and garden centres that are already in pots. If you want to grow plants from seed then you need pots, the right sort of soil, and seeds.

Go to the garden centre with your parents and have a chat with an assistant. The assistant will provide you with suitable soil and seeds or the plants you want.

Indoor gardening is a lot of fun. Houseplants bring colour and a feeling of summer to a room even in winter. Balconies can make good gardens in summer.

Growing Plants

Babies need a lot of care, love and help, whether they are human babies, animal babies or baby plants. Sunny the sunflower seed will tell you how tiring it is to grow.

"Hi! here I am again. Greetings to all gardeners.

"I'm pleased that you want to help me to become a big, proud sunflower. It's not easy, I can tell you.

"At first I need only a small pot, measuring about 10 centimetres across. Some sunflowers eventually grow much bigger, a lot bigger than you! I'm one of them.

"I might even grow taller than your teacher. So after a few weeks you will have to put me in a larger pot, because the old one will have become too small.

"You will see a drainage hole in the base of the pot. That's in case you give me too much water. The extra water drains out this hole. You should put a piece of broken earthenware over this hole so that soil doesn't drain out too. (Ask your parents for a piece.) Then comes the soil."

A little cucumber seedling reaching up to the light. The plant on the left has just emerged and is freeing itself from the seed's skin. The seed leaves can be seen clearly on the plant in the middle, and the plant on the right has already developed proper cucumber leaves.

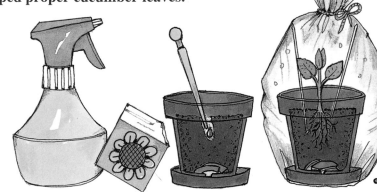

These pictures show how Sunny the Sunflower grows: Put him into the soil as a seed, and he will grow into a tender little seedling

"It's best to do this on the balcony or in the kitchen, just in case some soil spills - which often happens, even with adults! Now you have to dampen the soil.

"Now press me into the soil in the middle of the pot, about two or three centimetres deep. Put the pot into a clear plastic bag and put it on the window sill. You don't need to water me for a while. The plastic bag will stop the water evaporating, and right now I don't need much water. Indoor gardeners can sow me in March. Outdoor gardeners can sow me directly into the ground, but not until April, because it is too cold for me outside until then.

"You should realise that for seeds to sprout the temperature of the soil in the ground is more important than the temperature of the air. You have probably noticed that in winter the sun might shine quite brightly, while the ground is still frozen.

"The earth takes much longer than the air to warm up. This is true for all plants, not just for me. But don't put pots on top of a heater, as it is much too warm for them there.

"After a week, or perhaps a bit longer, you will see my first leaves, the seed-leaves. They push their way through the soil very slowly, on the end of a long stalk. At the same time I grow downwards, and my roots form.

"In a few days you will have to take off the plastic bag, because I need fresh air and water. The bigger I get, the more water I need. Light is also very important. But don't place me in direct sunlight yet, as my delicate leaves might burn. Later I will need lots of sun - after all, I am a sunflower!"

needing protection. Soon he needs a bigger pot, and now he is altogether grown up and bigger than you!

"I grow quite quickly, and so in about four weeks you will have to repot me into a bigger pot. It's not just young plants who have to change their 'rooms'. Older plants keep on growing and they too need a new pot every once in a while. Putting me into a new pot involves the same process as repotting all other plants. Listen carefully and I'll tell you how.

"You need to cover the drainage holes of bigger pots too. To make quite sure that not too much water collects in the bottom layer of soil, first put gravel in the pot, up to about two centimetres deep. This is called the drainage layer. Instead of gravel you can use beads, available from garden shops. The water drains out of the soil, trickles between the stones and runs out of the drainage hole.

"The soil layer goes on top of the gravel layer. Don't fill the pot completely. Now you have to move me to my new home.

"This is easiest if you place your left hand on top of my pot. Support the base of my stem by clamping it between your second and third finger. Hold the pot in your right hand and tip me up. I will fall into your hand together with the soil."

"If your hands are too small, ask an adult to help you. My root ball will have taken on the shape of the pot. This might remind you of making sandcastles. Now put me into the middle of the new pot. Fill the pot up with more soil, firming the soil up against me as you go. Don't press too hard. When you are repotting older plants you will see a lot of fine, white roots in the soil. These are just as important for plants as the leaves and flowers you see above ground. We plants use these roots to suck up water and nutrients that we need from the soil .

"Do you remember my story about the seed? There are lots of seeds much smaller than me. If you are sowing them you should put several in one pot. If you want to grow plants from very fine seeds then it's best to use special seed-raising boxes, which are available in garden centres. You

There is always plenty for a gardener to do. Young plants grow quickly and soon need a bigger pot, seedlings have to be pricked out (you'll find out how in the next few pages) and any plants you buy will have to be planted in the garden or on the balcony.

should also use seed-raising compost mix, a special soil suitable for seeds. It contains few nutrients because seeds are not very hungry.

"Fine seeds can be a problem. They must be spread evenly over the soil, and that's difficult. But I'll give you a tip. Take an old postcard or a similar piece of thin card and fold it in half. If you have very small hands, cut the postcard in half first. Shake some seeds into the 'V'.

"If you shake the postcard very carefully from side to side, and keep one end a little lower than the other, then only a few seeds will come out each time. You can practise shaking seeds like this by shaking raw semolina or rice on to a piece of paper in the kitchen, or shaking sand outside in a sandpit.

"Sprinkle a little fine soil over the seeds and press them gently into the soil using a small chopping board from the kitchen or a similar piece of wood. Now you need to water the seeds. A watering can won't do, because the water will come out too strongly and wash the seeds away. You need a mist spray. Your parents might have one for dampening clothes before ironing, or they might have one specially for plants. There is not much difference.

"If your parents have given you a little seed raising box then it

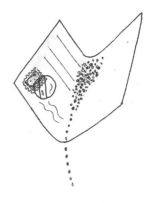

The postcard trick.

will probably have a clear hood. Use this to cover the box. It will now look rather like the glass coffin Snow White slept in!

"You must make sure that the soil doesn't get too cold. Some special seed-raising boxes have a built-in electric heating system which will keep the correct temperature. Most seeds like the temperature to be around 18-25°C. There are special thermometers with which you can measure the temperature in the soil.

"Underneath the hood the seeds will soon start to sprout. The moisture and warmth help them. If you keep seeds dry and cool then they stay as they are. Some can be kept for years and will still be capable of growing into a new plant."

Baby plants feel right at home in a mini-greenhouse, but make sure that they are not growing too close together.

"Although you'll be curious about what happens next, don't lift the hood yet. You can see your seed bed through the hood. After several days or even weeks - it depends on the plant - you will see a green fuzz on the soil. If you look closely you will see that this is made up of many tiny plants. These are the seedlings.

"Although plants look very different from each other when they are bigger, at this stage they all look the same. It is a good idea to stick a label or the empty seed packet on to the side of the box so that you don't forget what's inside.

"Usually the tiny seedlings are growing much too closely together and have to compete with each other for air, light and nutrients. By the time your baby plants are about four centimetres tall you will be able to tell which are strong ones and which are weak ones. You will have to say goodbye to the weak ones. Now remove the strong seedlings very carefully. This is called pricking out. Make sure that the fine roots don't break off. Another tip: loosen the soil with a toothpick or a small twig, and pick up the seedling by one of the upper leaves.

"You should have their new home ready before you start pricking out. This could be a pot or a plant tub.

Seedlings need plenty of space if they are to grow well - that's why you should prick them out and replant them.

Small pointed objects such as toothpicks, a pencil or a small spoon can help you to prick out and replant your seedlings. Tweezers can be useful too, as long as you take care not to squeeze them so hard that you squash the delicate seedlings.

It's fun to grow cress in a hedgehog dish like this.

Cress grows so quickly that you can almost see it getting bigger.

Once the cress is fully grown you can eat it.

"The plants now have a bigger appetite and need soil containing more nutrients. Don't forget the drainage layer of gravel or beads. Use a pencil to poke a hole in the soil and place the seedling in the hole. It should be planted up to the same depth it was before.

"The plants will stay in their new 'living room' for the rest of the growing season, so you have to work out how far apart they should be. Small plants like radishes need about 10 centimetres all around, a big plant might need a pot to itself. Usually the seed packet will tell you how much space the plant needs. If you follow the instructions you can't go wrong and each plant can develop beautifully.

"With your small hands you can carry out this process of pricking out much better than adults with their bigger hands. Be very gentle with the little plants, because they are as sensitive as all small organisms. The tiny roots are especially important, and most important of all are the outer, very fine roots. The plant uses these to suck up its food.

"The plants need to be watered in their new home. After a while they will need fertiliser, but not straight away, because shop-bought potting compost always contains fertilizer. So the plants need to 'eat up' these nutrients first. I'll tell you later about adding fertilizer.

"I know how impatient children are, so I'll give you the names of a few plants that won't keep you waiting long. I'm a fast grower - I grow to three metres in one summer. There are smaller versions of me which grow to only 40 centimetres.

"These plants will grow on a balcony or windowsill and take one to two weeks to sprout: Busy Lizzie, Canterbury Bells (campanula), ageratum, marigolds, chrysanthemums, Black-Eyed Susan, scarlet runner beans, tagetes, forget-me-not, ornamental corn, mimosa, coleus and zinnias.

"Perhaps you would like to grow healthy salad vegetables. Cucumbers grow quickly, as do radishes, many types of lettuce, and tomatoes. You can even make a little herb garden on your windowsill or balcony. Garden centres have kits complete with pots, seeds and soil. Cress is a lot of fun to grow. It doesn't even need soil, and will sprout on damp paper or cloth, in clay dishes shaped like animals and, of course, in soil. In three or four days the first plants appear, and you can cut them right away to add to a salad or to a sandwich with cream cheese or just butter. You can grow cress all through the year on your windowsill, and in summer you can grow it in the garden. Well, I've told you enough. I'll see you later in the garden. Bye!"

Sunny can grow on a windowsill, but he feels better outside. There are other plants which prefer to be inside. You will learn about them on the following pages.

Plants in a Room

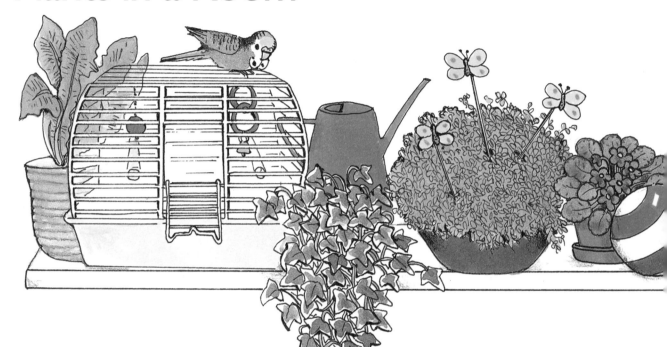

Make things easy for yourself. Avoid fussy and sensitive plants that don't like this and don't like that, that start to droop the minute you forget to water them, that have special needs and create a lot of work for you.

Although plants start out in the world as seeds, if you yourself are a beginner at gardening then it might be easier to ask for ready-grown plants. These can be bought at flower shops and garden centres. Busy Lizzies are fun to grow. They certainly deserve their name, since they bloom for long periods at a time.

The flowers can be white, red, pink or orange. Busy Lizzies like to live on the windowsill, but not in direct sun. How often you need to water them depends on the temperature in the room. If the room is very warm then you will need to water them more often than if it is cooler.

Every morning you should check your plants. Look carefully at the soil and feel it with your finger. If the soil looks and feels dry then you need to water the plant. Don't pour in too much water, because Busy Lizzies hate having wet feet. Every two weeks you should fertilise the plant. It isn't worthwhile buying fertilizer for just one plant, so ask your parents for some of the fertilizer they give their plants.

Spider Plants are also fun to grow, even though they don't have interesting flowers. Instead they grow baby Spider Plants. The plant is made up of long stalks, on the end of which grow mini Spider Plants. Some even have small, white roots under the baby plants. These stalks are called runners.

You can fit lots of plants on to a large windowsill. Make sure that you leave enough space so that you can water them easily.

You can leave the baby Spider Plants to grow on the end of the stalk, or you can cut them off and plant them in a pot. Then you will get a whole new Spider Plant. Why not try it? A baby plant that you have grown yourself makes a good present for a friend.

It is a good idea to place a Spider Plant on a shelf near the window where the long stalks can hang down, which looks very pretty.

Spider Plants need to be watered often so that the soil always feels damp (but not wet),

and they need to be fertilised every two weeks. Eventually a Spider Plant will outgrow its pot. You will know when, because the pot will seem to be fuller. This is because the roots will have grown and there won't enough room for them. You should then repot the Spider Plant into a pot about one or two centimetres bigger all around, using rich soil.

Do you know what Baby's Tears look like? They are related to stinging nettles, but don't sting and are much prettier. They have very small leaves and form a

round, green tuft. Baby's Tears aren't fussy, except about one thing: they don't like to be watered from above.

Keep the plant in a large saucer and pour the water into that. The water will be sucked up into the soil through the drainage holes. If any water is still in the saucer after an hour then you should carefully tip it out. When you can see the Baby's Tears' roots growing out through the drainage holes then it is time to repot it. Baby's Tears like to be fertilised every three weeks.

27

Flowering cactus.

Spider Plant.

Column Cactus.

African Violet.

Baby's Tears (Helxine).

African Violets have similar drinking habits to Baby's Tears. They too should be watered from below, because water leaves ugly brown marks on the leaves. If you are very careful and avoid getting water on the leaves then you can water them from above. It's easier if your watering can has a long,

narrow spout, because then you can rest the spout on the soil while you pour. African Violets don't like a lot of water and the surface layer of soil should feel dry. They like to be fertilised every three weeks.

African Violets have white, pink, violet, mauve or reddish flowers. Sometimes the edges of the petals are paler. You could collect African Violets of different colours. They like windowsills as long as they don't get too warm and are not in the sun all day.

Aspidistras are extremely hardy. They are sometimes called the 'cast iron plant', because you can put them almost anywhere. They don't need much light, don't mind the cold or heat, survive dusty air and draughts and don't need much water. Aspidistra is part of the plant's Latin name, Aspidistra elatior.

All plants have a scientific name, and this name often comes

from Latin, or sometimes Greek. Plants have a scientific name so that scientists from all over the world can use this name when they meet and talk about plants. Then they all know what plant they are talking about, even though the same plants may have different names in different parts of the world and in other languages.

But let's return to the aspidistra. Water it only when the top layer of soil feels quite dry. It needs to be fertilised every two weeks in summer but not at all in winter.

Succulents and cacti are easy to take care of. Succulents are the plants with the thick, fleshy leaves. Cacti have prickles - so watch out! It is fun and easy to grow these plants.

Aspidistra.

Money Tree.

Aloe.

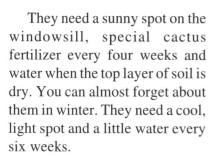

Busy Lizzie.

Prickly Pear (Opuntia).

They need a sunny spot on the windowsill, special cactus fertilizer every four weeks and water when the top layer of soil is dry. You can almost forget about them in winter. They need a cool, light spot and a little water every six weeks.

You will have to think about a suitable place for them. There might be space on a windowsill in a cooler room such as a bedroom or a storage room. There might be a good spot in the stairwell, providing that your parents or neighbours, if you live in a block of flats, don't mind. This period of winter rest is important for many plants. They stock up their energy reserves, ready to flower next year. Cacti must rest from October until March. In September give your cactus less water than usual, and in March gradually start to increase the amount of water again.

Cacti take various forms. Some look as if they have been stuck together out of oddly shaped bits and pieces. They usually belong to the Opuntia family. Some consist of several columns and others grow up high like a tower. Some are round like a ball. Have a look in the garden centre. Some cacti are as small as a thimble, while others are as big as a tree - at least they are in their native environment. Most indoor plants are not native to Europe. Most cacti come from Mexico, Argentina or from Texas in the USA.

Many cacti flower in summer. These are colourful flowers that are usually attached to the cactus like a star. A few grow on long stems.

Succulents are easy to care for and come in all sorts of odd shapes. Some sorts, such as Euphorbia, contain a poisonous sap - you should make sure that you don't buy them! The Aloe is attractive.

It has fat leaves that are marked with an interesting pattern. The Jade Plant is also a succulent. You might know it by some other name, such as Money Tree.

All succulents need a bright spot in your room, a little water, a little fertilizer every four weeks, and a winter rest like cacti.

Cuttings

Sometimes a branchlet breaks off a Jade Plant. Find a small jar in the kitchen, run some water into it, and place the branchlet in the jar so that most of it is above water. Small roots will start to grow from the base of the branchlet in a few days. Wait until the roots are about five centimetres long and then plant this cutting, as it is called, in a pot with fresh soil. And there you have it, a new plant! This works with some other plants too, such as Busy Lizzies.

You can even grow a new African Violet from a single leaf. Cut it off just above the ground and poke it into a small pot filled

Busy Lizzie cuttings will grow roots very quickly if put in a glass of water. Then you can plant the cutting in a pot.

You can grow hyacinths in a vase or in a pot with potting compost.

with damp potting compost. Up-end a big jar over the pot, or put the pot into a clear plastic bag and tie it tightly above the plant so that no air can escape. The sides of the jar or the plastic bag must not touch the leaf. Small roots will eventually form at the end of the stalk, but you won't be able to see them.

You won't know whether the experiment has worked or not until you see a tiny plant growing where the stalk enters the ground. When the plant has grown big and strong

you should repot it into a bigger pot with rich soil.

Until now we have talked only about flowers and plants with roots. There are also plants that grow from bulbs. Onions are a type of bulb. Many other plants grow from bulbs and these include tulips, daffodils, crocuses and snow-drops. They all grow in the garden.

Hyacinths flower in spring when they grow outside in the garden, but they will flower in winter if you grow them inside on the windowsill. This is called 'forcing' them.

Garden centres and flower shops sell hyacinth bulbs in autumn. You need a special vase and a little pointed paper hat to put on top of a hyacinth bulb.

A hyacinth vase looks rather like a little dish sitting on top of a glass. The vase should be filled with water up to the base of the dish. Place the hyacinth bulb on top of the dish. The bulb shouldn't touch the water; there should be about half a centimetre between them. Now put the little hat on top of the bulb and place the whole thing in a dark room for several weeks.

Every once in a while you should check that there is enough water in the vase, and add more water if necessary. Make sure that no water runs over the bulb. You should start this in early October. You will notice that lots of long, white, smooth roots will start growing from the base of the bulb. The more roots the better. In early December bring the vase into a warmer room, perhaps a bedroom. After a few days you can put the hyacinth on the windowsill. The hat should stay on for a while yet. Eventually shoots will appear from the top of the bulb and push up the hat. You can remove the hat when they are about eight centimetres long. The shoots will look rather pale at first, but they will soon become greener. Soon you will be able to make out leaves and a flower stem. Your hyacinth should bloom in time for Christmas. Hyacinths in bloom have a lovely fragrance and make a good present.

You can also grow hyacinths in a pot in potting compost. A pot measuring about 12 centimetres across would be suitable. Fill it with normal potting compost and plant the hyacinth deep enough so that only its tip shows. Water it a little and then put a box over the

You can grow a new African Violet from just one leaf.

pot. The pot has to rest in a cool place for several weeks. Check it once in a while and make sure that the soil is a little damp. In early December you can bring it into a

slightly warmer place, and then into your room. Leave the box over it, or put a little hat over the tip, and leave it there until the shoot is about 12 centimetres long. After that treat it just like a hyacinth in a vase.

If your parents have a garden then you can plant the hyacinth bulb outside after it has finished flowering, but you will have to wait until April. Until then you must look after the bulb, even when it doesn't look pretty any more. Continue to water it regularly and fertilise it every three weeks. The hyacinth will bloom again next spring.

This is how to 'force' a hyacinth bulb in a hyacinth vase: The bulb has to wear a hat at first. Leaves gradually develop and eventually the fragrant bloom appears.

The Balcony

If you take the time to arrange things just right then you can make a proper little garden on a balcony or terrace. The plants can grow in flower boxes, in tubs or in troughs.

Plants that grow on a balcony are not usually the same as plants that grow indoors. They are outdoor plants. Some of them are easier to grow than others. Young gardeners will probably prefer flowers that grow quickly - like the sunflower. Sunny the sunflower seed can grow into a beautiful flower on a balcony. First, check with your parents that your balcony is strong enough to hold tubs. Then ask which flower boxes you can use, or in which corner of the balcony you can put your trough or tub. It is best not to change your mind, because troughs and tubs are heavy and hard to move around.

There are lots of ways to turn a balcony into a garden paradise. Even Sunny feels quite at home on a balcony.

A tub like this is big enough for a beautiful little flower garden.

Flower boxes have drainage holes too, and these must be covered with pieces of broken earthenware. You then need to put in a drainage layer of broken earthenware, beads or gravel, just as you did with indoor plants. This will stop the plants from getting wet feet. If you are growing summer flowers then use normal potting compost, which is available at garden centres.

Many plants are sold in spring as baby plants. Try to visit a garden centre or nursery with your parents. The baby plants won't look very interesting, but don't let that put you off. Buds and flowers will all come later - if you look after them.

Leave plenty of space between the young plants when you plant them out to allow for growth. Although they look lonely and miserable now there will be a mass of blooms in the summer.

You will need a bigger plant box to set up a proper vegetable garden.

Peas, beans and vines need a frame to climb up.

What plants would be suitable for your first garden on a balcony? Daisies are fun. They come in various colours: white, pink and red. Each plant needs about 10 centimetres to spread out. Daisies can be planted out in March or later.

Daisies look pretty next to forget-me-nots, which come in various shades of blue, from dark blue to light blue.

Plants grown on balconies need to be fertilised regularly and given enough water.

Pansies are another possibility. Winter-flowering pansies can be planted in October, and will flower until the spring. They don't mind getting cold, and are available in all sorts of colours.

How often you have to water your plants depends on the temperature and how much rain they get. Plants are similar to you in that they get thirsty if it's warm and they're left standing around in the sun all day. If they are being rained on you won't have to water them so much.

Balcony plants won't need any fertilizer for the first six weeks because there is enough fertilizer in the soil. Gradually they will eat up the nutrients, and then you will have to add more.

Liquid fertilizer is the easiest sort to use - you just add it to the water in the watering can. Follow the directions on the packet about how much to use, and remember that too much fertilizer will make plants sick.

The balcony gardener has to do more than just water and fertilise the plants. One task arises when flowers start to wilt, as they always do. That doesn't look very nice in a balcony garden, so you should cut off flowers as soon as they start to fade. Yellow leaves should be removed too.

Every once in a while the soil needs to be loosened. There are special hand forks and trowels

Cut off wilted flowers and yellow leaves as soon as you notice them. This will help the plant to produce new flowers.

suitable for this, which you will have read about in the chapter on garden equipment. Dig the soil very carefully. You must avoid disturbing the roots, so don't dig too deep.

Daisies, forget-me-nots and pansies don't bloom all summer, so in May you might want to change the plants in your flower box. Blue ageratum, antirrhinum, begonias, marguerites, lobelia, fragrant stock, tagetes and portulacas will all flower until autumn.

Some balconies don't get much sun, in which case you must choose your flowers carefully. You see, most flowers need a lot of sun.

There are two very pretty plants that do like a shady spot. You know one already: Busy Lizzie. This is an indoor plant but it will grow on a balcony as well. Fuchsias also enjoy the shade. Its flowers hang down from the branches like little bells.

So far we have talked about flowering plants that you can buy as seedlings, but you can also sow seed in your balcony garden. Nasturtiums are easy to grow from seed. They grow quickly, have attractive round leaves, and big orange flowers, and flower all through the summer. There are some interesting climbing plants, such as dwarf scarlet runner beans and fragrant vetch.

Some plants can't be planted until all danger of frost is past, which is usually in mid-May. They include the Morning Glory (Convulvulus), Black-Eyed Susan and other summer flowers.

You can of course also grow a herb garden on a balcony. Your family would be sure to enjoy fresh chives and parsley in salads. Both of these kitchen herbs will grow even in half shade and they like damp soil. Thyme, rosemary and marjoram will grow only in sun. They don't need much water and don't need any fertilizer.

Vegetables can be grown in a flower box or other large container. Try growing tomatoes, for example cherry tomatoes.

Cherry tomatoes.

Alpine strawberries.

They are only slightly bigger than cherries and taste wonderful. If you want to grow radishes or carrots then use a deep box, because radishes and carrots are roots, and they need room to grow fat and long. It's logical really!

You need special, chemical-free soil to grow vegetables, and you should use only organic fertilisers (made from seaweed or dried blood-and-bone, for example).

If you have a sweet tooth then you might enjoy growing straw-berries. Alpine strawberries grow particularly well in pots and boxes. They are related to wild straw-berries, and their tiny berries are delicious. They need rich earth containing compost. Plant them in early spring and the first berries should be ripe by June.

You can even grow a little apple tree in a pot on the balcony. And it will bear real apples! Mini

apple trees are grown in special nurseries and sold in large pots.

Fruit and vegetables need to be watered regularly. They are really garden plants, because they enjoy having plenty of space and their roots can spread out to search for water and nutrients. They don't really have enough room in a pot or box, and they use up water and nutrients quickly. So they need special care if they are to do well.

Don't expect a bumper harvest from your crop. Every single tomato and strawberry is an achievement to be proud of - and to enjoy!

Light, Air, Warmth, Water

Each leaf is a miracle of nature, a tiny factory producing sugar, starch and oxygen. Water from the soil and carbon dioxide from the air are the raw materials. Chlorophyll (the green colour in leaves) does all the work, and the energy to power it comes from sunlight.

Young gardeners might find this all rather mysterious. But the work that leaves do is very

Plants provide air for us to breathe. A leaf breathes in carbon dioxide through tiny...

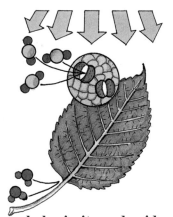

... holes in its underside, and breathes out oxygen.

important, not just for the plant itself, but also for all other living things in the world, including animals and humans.

Their work can be explained like this: There are tiny openings on the underside of a leaf. A leaf uses these to breathe in carbon dioxide. The chlorophyll converts the carbon dioxide into carbon and oxygen. The plant then breathes out most of the oxygen, which is just as well for us and other animals, since we need oxygen to live.

The plant uses a small proportion of the oxygen itself, and then there is just carbon and hydrogen left in the leaf 'factory'. The plant uses these to make carbohydrates in the form of glucose, which is later turned into starch. This process is called assimilation. It allows some plants to produce things like potatoes!

You see, the products of assimilation don't just sit around in the leaves doing nothing. In the case of potatoes, the starchy end product collects in the roots.

Some plants need more energy -

or sunlight - than others to carry out all this work. That's why some plants grow only in sun, and others in shade. This whole process has a lovely long name: photosynthesis.

Apart from light and air, plants also need warmth at particular stages of their life. As you know, a seed needs warmth to sprout and then to grow. Later on plants need warmth so that their fruit can ripen and their seeds can develop.

As with energy, some plants need more warmth than others. Flowers, trees and shrubs living in the British Isles must be able to adapt to the climate, which can be hot or cold, wet or dry. Tomatoes, peppers and peaches need plenty of warmth to ripen, while some plants, like the beautiful dahlia, cannot stay outside in winter.

One more thing is important: water. Plants have roots so that they can absorb water. The ends of the roots are very fine and have the most important job in the whole root system.

They are continuously searching for water. They dig deep into the ground and absorb water.

The green chlorophyll in leaves and the energy of the sun work to turn water (from rain) and carbon dioxide (from the air breathed out by people and animals) into oxygen, sugar and starch.

That's why it is so important to handle these fine roots carefully when you are planting or repotting plants. Water helps plants in many ways. For example it dissolves nutrients and carries them around the plant. Much of the water collected by the roots evaporates through the leaves and keeps the temperature around the plant even.

The same thing happens to humans: you become thirsty when it is warm because water evaporates through your skin. This is what is happening when you sweat. Sweating is very important in keeping your body cool and ensures that you don't suffer from heat stroke. If it is cold then you don't feel so thirsty.

The roots of plants are quite clever. Do you remember Wiggle the Worm? Roots like to grow along the little tunnels made by rain-worms in the soil. Not only is it easier for them to stretch out along the tunnels, but they can also feast on the nutritious worm droppings that line the tunnel walls.

Nutrients

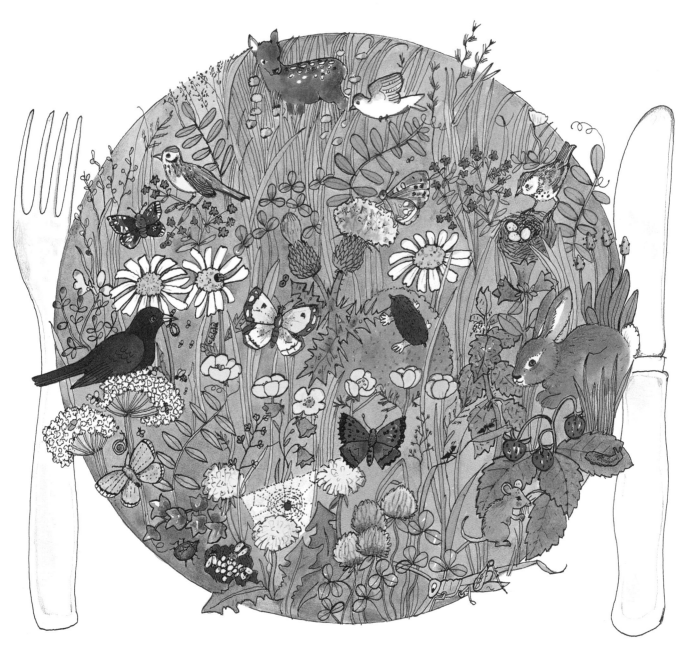

A biotope is a community of plants and animals, which acts as a home for all its members. They each have somewhere to live and can find something to eat, and in return they each have a job to do.

Some plants are heavy feeders while others are light feeders, and their tastes vary too, just like people and animals.

The system works well in wilderness areas where there are not many people to interfere. Whether it is in a field, in a pine forest or in a deciduous woodland - made up of trees that drop their leaves in autumn - only those plants that like each others' company grow next to each other. Either they like the same sort of soil or they provide each other with what they need.

You shouldn't pick flowers or fruit from wilderness areas because all the petals, leaves, dead twigs and fruit are needed. They fall on to the ground and provide food for the animals and micro-organisms living in the soil. The animals convert the plant material into nutrients for the soil.

Wild animals belong to the natural system. Birds, deer, hares and many other animals feed from plants. This natural, functioning system is called a biotope. You have probably heard this word already. A biotope is a community of plants and animals.

A functioning biotope provides the right quantities of the right nutrients. Your garden, balcony and pot plants aren't biotopes, so you have to help them. After all, you want to eat your strawberries and tomatoes, not leave them to rot on the ground as fertilizer! There is a lot less room in flower pots and other containers than in a garden, and worms rarely wriggle their way into pots. You might be wondering what plant nutrients look like.

Some of them are invisible. Let's start with nitrogen. It is a gas and there is plenty of it around - the air is 78% nitrogen. The scientific symbol for nitrogen is 'N'. Scientific symbols are often used on fertilizer packets. So if you see '12%N' on a fertilizer packet, you know that the fertilizer contains 12 per cent nitrogen. So far so good.

Plants need nitrogen so that their leaves will grow and turn green. Plants can suck nitrogen out of the air, and some plants manage to do this so well that they have more nitrogen than they need, which they then deposit in the soil. They are called legumes and include peas, beans, vetch and lupins.

How do they manage to do this? A special sort of bacteria (not all bacteria are harmful) live on the roots of legumes. The nitrogen is sucked in from the air and the bacteria store it in nodules attached to the roots.

When the leaves need nitrogen the plant sends some up from the nodules. Usually there is a lot of nitrogen left over in the nodules, and so when you are clearing away wilted peas or beans in autumn you should leave the nitrogen-rich roots in the ground. Whatever plant grows there next year will find plenty of nitrogen in the soil.

Many gardeners make use of the work legumes do by sowing lupins. They cut the lupins just before or just after flowering, leaving the roots in the ground. The cut-off stalks and leaves go onto the compost heap. The soil is hoed lightly. All the nodules of nitrogen stay in the ground, and whatever plant comes next will have a real feast!

Gardeners call this process green manuring, which means that green plants are used as fertilizer. Nitrogen is also created by dead plant and animal matter rotting in the ground.

There is another sort of fertilizer that contains nitrogen: animal manure. You sometimes still see manure heaps in farmyards. You might even see a cockerel crowing on top of one! The manure heap is made up of straw and animal manure, which is why it doesn't smell too good. Farmers spread the contents of their manure heap over their fields at least once a year, usually in autumn.

You can still find a real dung-heap in many farmyards.

Lupins store nitrogen in little nodules on their roots.

You might be pleased to know that you don't need to build a manure heap in your garden. You can buy manure in bags, and you can even get dried, powdered cow manure that doesn't smell. You can also buy liquid manure in bottles. Some types are called 'guano' and these are made from the droppings of sea birds and fish waste. You can buy dried blood and bone by the bag - it too is rich in nitrogen.

You might think that this is all a bit yucky, but animal manure is not yucky in the right place. It helps to make the soil nutritious and healthy, whether in your garden or in a wood.

A few words of warning: while plants do like nitrogen they don't like too much of it. It might make them grow very quickly, but their leaves will be soft and floppy, and likely to be attacked by pests or disease - more about that later. If, on the other hand, plants are not getting enough nitrogen then they will mope about and not grow properly.

Nitrogen has a property that can be dangerous. The form of nitrogen that plants eat is nitrate, a salt. It can collect in leaves, for example in lettuce or spinach. In small quantities it is harmless. But too much nitrate can make people ill, especially babies.

Phosphorous is another nutrient that all plants need. It is found in the soil as phosphoric acid, or salt. This is called phosphate. Its scientific abbreviation is 'P'.

Plants need phosphorous to produce flowers. They also need it to form fruit, seed, and strong roots. There is always enough phosphorous in healthy soil containing plenty of earthworms. You almost never need to use a special phosphate fertilizer, because it is usually added to nitrogen fertilisers just in case. Guano and bone meal contain a lot of phosphate. Phosphate is a waste product from iron smelters. It is found naturally in some iron ore. When the iron ore is melted down, slag rich in phosphate is produced. This slag is then finely ground.

Both too much and too little phosphorous will prevent plants from growing properly and will result in a small harvest of fruit and vegetables.

Plants also need potassium. It is abbreviated to 'K'. A healthy soil usually contains as much potassium as plants need. Potassium makes plants strong and able to stand up to gusts of wind. It also helps to make fruit taste good, and makes roots and tubers strong.

Animal manure contains a lot of potassium. Too much potassium prevents the organisms living in the soil from doing their job properly, and this will make plants grow badly. Too little potassium prevents them from growing much at all.

Lime (abbreviated to 'C') is also important, as it too makes plants strong. There are various sorts of lime fertilizer. If you have your own patch of garden then your parents will probably fertilise it with lime if necessary.

You might already have heard of the pH value. The pH value tells you how acidic or alkaline soil is. Soil low in lime is acid, and has a low pH value. Soil high in lime is alkaline, and has a high pH value.

There is one more thing that plants need, and that is magnesium (abbreviated to 'Mg'). Plants need this to produce chlorophyll, the green colour of leaves. It is safer to ask your parents to fertilise your garden with magnesium.

In addition to these basic nutrients, plants need iron, copper, zinc, manganese and other nutrients, but in such tiny quantities that you can't see them or weigh them on a normal set of scales. The soil contains no more than a trace of them, which is why they are called trace elements.

Now you're in for a surprise. You need these trace elements too, and you need lime (which is the same as calcium), phosphorous, magnesium, and lots of the other things that plants need. Iron is found in meat and many sorts of vegetables, calcium is found in milk products, and phosphorous in fish.

Cows help to keep the cycle of nature going: they eat grass and then fertilise the field with their dung.

The basic principle of all this is simple. A healthy, nutritious, disease-free soil will grow healthy plants for you or animals to eat. This keeps the animals healthy and means that their meat is nutritious. All this helps to keep you fit and healthy. You will know now how important the earth and earthworms and all the other organisms living in the soil are. If they did not exist then there would be no plants, no animals and no people.

Fertilizer is available in garden centres, but you can make some for yourself too. If you have a balcony garden or indoor plants

Plants like nothing better than a cup of cold tea.

then it might not be worthwhile making fertilizer just for them, because you will need only small quantities. However there are some waste products from the kitchen that you can use. You can add leftover tea (black or herbal) to the watering can every four weeks. Used ground coffee is good for plants too. Dig about a teaspoonful per pot into the surface of the soil. Use this more for tubs and flower boxes. Fertilizer sticks are a very conv-

Gardeners can make use of some of the things that other people throw away. A teaspoonful of used ground coffee is good for your plants. The rest of the coffee, together with the paper filter, can be thrown on the compost heap.

enient method of fertilising indoor plants. They contain all the necessary nutrients in the correct quantities. Read the instructions on the packet to find out how many sticks to use. It will depend on the size of the pot and the quantity of soil. There are different sorts of fertilizer sticks for different plants: flowering plants, for example, need a different sort to non-flowering plants.

There are a few basic rules about fertilising:

* Never fertilise plants when the soil is dry.
* Most indoor plants need fertilizer only between March and October.
* If you add liquid fertilizer to the watering can then don't splash water on the leaves. If they do get splashed, wipe the leaves imme-diately, or they will develop brown marks.
* The hotter it is, the more often you should fertilise and water plants.
* If rain falls on your plants then it will wash away the fertilizer. You will probably have to add more.
* If your plants have yellow leaves and are not producing any buds, then they probably need fertilizer.
* If the leaves on your plants are soft and droopy, then they probably need water.

Stinging nettles are very nutritious, and nettle tea is simple to make and it is a good fertilizer.

Nettle tea is a natural and nutritious fertilizer that you can make from stinging nettles. Nettles do sting, but they are not harmful in any other way. They can do a lot of good, because they are rich in nitrogen.

Ask your parents if you can borrow an old plastic bucket or tub.

You will also need to wear an old pair of gloves so that you can pick the nettles without being stung. Nettles grow everywhere - perhaps there are some in a corner of your garden. You will need about one kilogram. Put the nettles in the bucket and pour 10 litres of water over them. If you have a rainwater supply use rainwater. Cover the bucket and leave it for several days, by which time it will probably smell bad. Your wonder-fertilizer will be ready in two weeks.

Nettle tea must be diluted before it is given to plants. This means that you will have to learn to measure accurately. Find an old container, like a yoghurt pot. Ask an adult to help you to measure 100 millilitres of water into it. Mark the water line on the pot then throw away the water. Now use the pot to measure 100 millilitres of nettle tea. Add this to two litres of water, and there you have your own fertilizer! Use this diluted nettle tea to water your plants in the normal way.

Plants need a fertilizer like nettle tea only once every four or five weeks. It's probably not worth making nettle tea just for your patch in the garden, so perhaps your parents would like to fertilise their part of the garden with nettle tea too - ask them first. You can read more in another chapter about how plant teas can also be used to protect plants from pests.

At some stage in autumn you will have harvested all your vegetables and all your flowers will have wilted. Then you should ask your parents for some compost. A small patch of garden needs about two bucketfuls, which should be spread over the ground and hoed into the surface layer of soil. Add some plant waste from the garden, such as leaves and dead stalks. Your garden can stay like this until spring. Much of the plant waste will have disappeared by then, thanks to the hard work of the organisms living in the soil, which will spend the winter producing humus.

Nettle tea.

Outside

A garden is a wonderful place. You can play in a garden, enjoy the fresh air, read, doze, do your homework, have parties and talk with your friends. A large part of your family life can take place in the garden as long as it is warm and the sun is shining. Toddlers and small children can have a lovely time in a sandpit or even a paddling pool, if it is warm enough. (But remember: an adult should always be there if you are using a pool.) Older children can enjoy playing badminton and ball games on the lawn.

What about the rest of the garden? What about the flower-beds, the bushes and the vegetable garden? Take a close look and you will see all sorts of interesting things. Let's go and discover your garden!

There are some corners that are almost always shady, where it will be pleasantly cool on scorching hot days. The bushes and trees and flowers growing there don't need much sun. You might find violets, ferns, lily-of-the-valley and wood anemones - if your parents have planted them. Sometimes wild plants that you would otherwise find in a wood start growing in these shady corners. Ask your parents whether they know the names of these plants. If they don't know, pick a leaf and a flower, if the plant has one, and take it to your science teacher at school.

Some parts of the garden get sun almost all day long - if it's shining, that is. Quite different plants grow there, usually only those that your parents have planted. You might find roses, antirrhinums, larkspur and our old friend the sunflower.

Each type of flower is different. The petals are a different colour and shape, the leaves are set on the stalks in different places. Some flowers are as brightly coloured as paints in a paintbox. Collect one bloom from each type of flower and one leaf from each bush and tree. Lay them all out on a table and compare them, and you will see how different they all are. Perhaps you can help your parents to look after the garden. They can show you how to use a spade properly and how to hoe the soil. And of course you will need to learn what is a weed and what is not.

That's difficult, because baby plants look very similar. But you have to learn, because how else can you weed the vegetable garden? Vegetables need room to grow and plenty of nutrients, so the weeds have to go. The radishes, carrots, lettuce and tomatoes will thank you for your work by growing big and strong. You could also help with watering and with tying tall flowers to stakes.

There's always something to do in a garden.

On a sunny day a garden is the best playground in the world.
Spielplatz der Welt

Your own patch

Of course it's a lot more fun to have your own patch of garden where you can do what you like. Ask your parents if you might have your own plot.

Did you have a sandpit in the garden when you were little? If the sandpit is still there, and no-one is using it, you could turn it into your own garden. Old sandpits make great gardens. You see, plants have similar needs to small children. A sandpit is usually in a sunny spot sheltered from the wind. That's good for small children and for plants as well. Sandpits are usually close to the house, so that parents can keep an eye on their children - or for you to keep an eye on your plants!

Your patch of garden shouldn't be wider than 60 centimetres, because if it's any wider you won't be able to reach into the middle easily. And it shouldn't be longer than one metre. That is really plenty of garden to begin with. If you really enjoy gardening this year, then you might be given more space next year.

It is a good idea to lay old wooden planks along the edges of

It is best to get an adult to fork over the ground first, then you rake the soil until it is smooth.

your plot. These make it much easier to walk and stand beside your garden without treading in it. And they offer a mud-free path when it rains.

Now what do you need to do? For a start you need to dig the ground, and to do that you need your parents' help. The ground should be broken up by digging with a garden fork. Digging forks don't usually come in children's size, so you will have to ask an adult to do this. It is very important to fork over the ground, as this makes it much easier for the roots to reach out into the soil. You can do the next task, which is to rake over the soil surface until it is smooth. Ask your parents before you begin whether you need to sprinkle any fertilizer over the soil, because the raking mixes the fertilizer into the soil.

46

You should then water the whole garden with a watering can or a garden hose. If you use a hose then turn the nozzle to a gentle spray. The water will help to wash the fertilizer into the soil.

Before you start all this, look at what you're wearing. Gardening often makes you sweat, and gets you dirty too, so it's not very sensible to go out into the garden wearing your best clothes. You need sturdy shoes, not sandals, which let in soil and water. You should wear a T-shirt and an old cotton shirt or a jumper on top.

On cold days you need an old jacket. Your parents might have old gardening clothes hanging up somewhere. Why don't you keep your gardening clothes there too?

The soil is all ready. Now comes the big moment when you have to decide what to plant! Sit down at the table with your parents and draw your plot of garden on a big piece of paper. If your garden is 60 centimetres wide and 100 centimetres long then make the drawing half as big: 30 centimetres wide and 50 centimetres long. Use different colours - red for radishes, green for lettuce, orange for carrots and so on - and draw in the plants.

Make sure that they are far enough apart. If you find this too complicated, ask your parents to help you. Your garden could look really attractive if, for example,

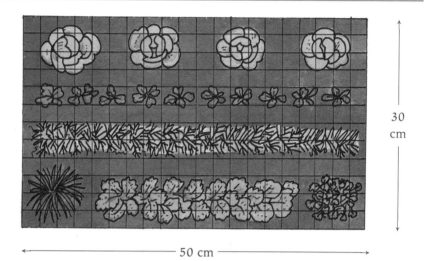

Your plan for a vegetable patch might look something like this . . .

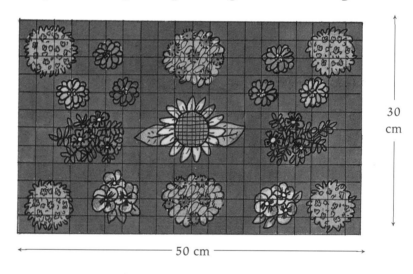

. . . and a colourful flower patch might be planned like this.

you plant vegetables in the middle and lettuce around the edges.

Be sure to arrange the plants so that they are next to their friends. This is called companion planting. Plants are like people in that they get on well with some plants and not so well with others. They

prefer to sit next to their friends. You can read more about this in the chapter about mixed cropping.

Seeds

Have you decided? Do you know what you want to grow in your garden? Yes? Well then, the first thing to do is to check the calender or to look out the window. April is usually the time to start gardening, but April in one place might be very different to April in another. It is colder in the north than in the south. So in April it is colder in Inverness (the North) than it is in Bournemouth (the South).

You can judge for yourself whether or not April where you live is warm enough to sow seeds. Look around in other gardens: can you see primroses, are the yellow forsythia and cherry trees in bloom? Are there dandelions in the fields and along the roadsides, and bluebells in the woods? Are the chestnut trees unfolding their leaves? If you can say yes to at least some of these questions, then you can start gardening.

Your plot of garden is all ready. Let's say you want to sow radishes, carrots and some kind of lettuce. There are many different varieties of lettuce, including some that you never see in the supermarket or at the vegetable market. Why don't you try growing an unusual kind? Mesclun, or Lamb's lettuces is fun to grow. It doesn't form a round head of leaves like most lettuces. Instead, small bunches of leaves grow directly out of the soil and look like lots of small rabbit's ears. Not all vegetables can be sown yet - some, such as beans and tomatoes, have to wait until May.

Now you need a length of string, two short sticks and a measuring stick or tape. Tie one end of the string to one of the sticks, and push it firmly into the ground on one of the shorter sides of the garden bed. Put it in about 10 centimetres from the long edge. Take the other end of the string and the other stick to the other end. Put the stick into the ground exactly opposite the first one. Now tie the loose end of string around this stick. Pull the string taut so that it runs above the ground. Now take a third stick and pull this along the string from one end to the other, letting it trail in the soil. This forms a narrow furrow, a drill, in the soil. And this is where the seeds go!

You can now move the sticks and the string. Move the sticks 20 centimetres further into the bed. Tie the string to both ends again and make another seed drill. You need three drills altogether. The drill in the middle should be shallow, about half a centimetre

A stretched-out piece of string will help you to make straight seed drills.

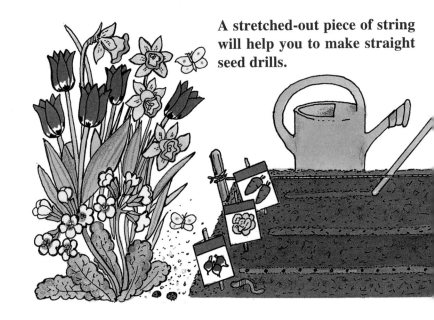

deep, while the first and the third drills should be one to two centimetres deep.

The radishes go into the first drill. Place a seed in the drill at one end. Measure seven centimetres, and place another seed in the drill. Measure seven centimetres again, and put in another seed, and so on. The radish seeds should be planted about one centimetre deep. Now they need to be covered. Use your fingertips to gently brush soil over each seed. You might as well leave the rest of the seed drill uncovered. That way you can see where the seeds are. An even better idea is to sprinkle some sand along the seed drill, when you have covered it over. This will stay there for a few days, which is useful, because

Seeds of different plants can look very different.

even radishes, which sprout very quickly, stay invisible for a week or more.

Sow Lamb's lettuces along the middle drill. Lamb's lettuces seed is very fine, so you might want to try using a postcard (have a look on page 23 if you have forgotten how). Let the seeds trickle thinly into the seed drill as you move the folded postcard along. Carefully brush a little soil over the seeds - it really just needs to cover them and no more. Lamb's lettuces are small plants and don't have the strength to push their way through a mound of soil. Mark this row with some sand too. You should see the first green tips in about a week.

And now for the third row: carrots. Use the postcard again and sow the seeds thinly. Carrots take a long time to sprout, so you won't see anything for about four weeks. That will really test your patience!

To make sure that you remember where your carrots are until they sprout you can sow a radish seed every 20 centimetres along the seed drill in with the carrots. Radishes sprout much sooner than carrots, and so they will show you where you can expect to see the carrots. Once the carrots have sprouted you can pull out the radishes - after all, you have another whole row of them.

After you have covered the carrot seeds all the seed drills need to be watered. Use a watering can with a very fine head, or a hose which can be turned to mist. A strong jet of water would wash the seeds away.

The radishes are already spaced correctly, but you will have to thin out the carrots and the Lamb's lettuces. Lamb's lettuces should be one centimetre apart, carrots three centimetres. Pull out all the extra seedlings when they are about five centimetres high. This is very important! Carrots need space to become fat and crunchy, and if they are too crowded then they will stay small and skinny. The Lamb's lettuces need space to develop nice green leaves.

Of course, you might want to grow something different. It is a good idea to have the drawing of your garden plot on the ground beside you as you sow. Write on the drawing how deep each type of seed needs to be sown.

If you are feeling lazy and your parents are feeling generous you could ask them to buy you seeds set in tape or made into pellets. This is a more expensive way of buying seeds, but it saves you the work of thinning out. It's also very practical.

Seeds set in tape are spaced as they would be after thinning.

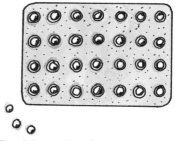

Seed in pellet form . . .

. . . is easy to sow.

These tapes of seeds are sold either with only one sort of vegetable in each tape, or with a variety of vegetables in each tape. You lay the tape in the seed drill and do everything else just as you would for normal seeds from a packet. The paper rots away under the soil. Seeds in pellet form are made by coating the seed with a special fertilizer. They may look like pills or sweets, but they are not, and may be poisonous, so be sure not to eat them by mistake! Seeds in pellet form can be spaced in the ground as they would be after thinning. They make sowing seeds much easier, especially fine seeds like carrot or lettuce.

Spring weather can be quite changeable. You might decide to go out for a walk on a lovely sunny day, and by the time you're ready to leave it has turned cold.

Carrots need to be thinned out properly if they are to grow big and fat.

This isn't a great problem, because all you have to do is run back inside and pull on a jumper.

Unfortunately for plants, they can't do this when the temperature drops. You can help to keep them warm by covering them with a sort of blanket. A plant blanket is made of thin plastic and has lots of tiny holes so that rain and air can get though to the plants. Perhaps your parents have one of these. If you hear on the weather forecast that frost is expected you can spread the blanket over your plants. The edges of the blanket have to be weighed down with stones so that it won't blow away in the wind. There are other ways of protecting plants from the cold. There are plastic tunnels and mini greenhouses, or you can sow the seeds in a big greenhouse and plant them out later. Ask your parents what they do, or visit a market garden.

Sometimes there isn't room in the garden to sow all the seeds in the packet and some are left over. Your parents will probably keep these. Before you use seeds from a previous year you should check that they are still fresh, as they don't stay fresh for ever. To test the

Perforated plastic.

freshness of seeds, lay about six layers of kitchen paper towel on a flat plate, dampen the paper and scatter a few seeds over the paper. Cover the plate with plastic film and put the plate in a warm, light spot (but not in the sun). The seeds should begin to sprout in a few days. If at least half the seeds sprout then the seeds are fresh enough to use. If only a few have sprouted then it would be a waste of time sowing them in the garden and you should throw the rest of them away.

Radishes, Lamb's lettuces and carrots can be sown in April. Other vegetables you could sow in April include silver beet, spinach, curly endive, peas, and all types of lettuce. If you want to be able to make really tasty salads over the summer then

A plastic tunnel.

you should try growing chives, parsley and dill. They can be planted in April too.

May weather can be very unpredictable, depending on where you live. Ask your parents whether they think there could still be a late frost. If there is going to be a frost, then it will probably be at the full moon, so if you're not sure, wait until after the full moon before you sow beans, cucumbers and courgettes (zucchini).

Taped seeds are very practical to use, as the seeds are already spaced correctly.

Planting Out

If you don't want to sow seeds, you can plant out seedlings. Many types of vegetables and flowers are available as seedlings.

Prepare your patch of garden exactly as you would to sow seeds. You won't need to make seed drills, but you do need to mark on the soil where you want to plant the seedlings. Be sure that you buy the seedlings on a day when you can plant them, because seedlings don't like being in boxes, and they will start to look very sad if they have to wait for days and days.

Each seedling needs a hole in the soil. Ask your parents if they have a dibble. If they don't, a short, thick stick with a pointed end will do. Look at your seedlings: how long are their roots?

Bore a hole in the soil, deep enough so that all the roots can hang downwards. They shouldn't poke up through the soil. The seedling should sit in the hole at the same depth as it sits in its box. The soil should come up as far as the spot where the stem begins. Hold the seedling with your left hand so that it is at the right height inside the hole, and then push some soil into the hole. Press the soil in gently, so that there are no

Courgettes (zucchini).

empty spaces and the seedling is sitting firmly, not flopping over.

Some seedlings have so many roots that you will need to dig a hole with a hand trowel. Dig the hole as big and as deep as necessary, and plant the seedling in the hole along with any soil stuck to its roots.

Pumpkin.

When you are planting out you need to make sure that you space the seedlings far enough apart. You must also check that you are planting out seedlings at the right time of the year. Kohlrabi and leeks can be planted in April. Lettuce can be planted in early May. Tomatoes, cucumber and pumpkin can only be planted when all danger of frost is past. If you want to grow a pumpkin - and one pumpkin is really enough - you will need more space, because one pumpkin plant needs one square metre of ground all to itself. It would take up the whole of your garden plot, and growing nothing but one pumpkin plant would be boring! Pumpkins are very hungry plants and need plenty of compost, so it is wise to grow them near the compost heap, where possible.

Cucumbers need lots of space too: they should be 50 centimetres apart. Pumpkins belong to the same family as cucumbers and zucchini, and they are all easy to grow from seed. Plant two seeds of each in little pots on your windowsill in April. By late May they will have grown into strong plants and you can plant them out.

So far you have learnt how to sow seeds and plant out seedlings.

Garlic is grown differently. Cloves of garlic can be planted in April. Plant them 15 centimetres apart and five centimetres deep, and with the tip pointing upwards.

Gardening is even more fun when friends, brothers and sisters help.

53

Bucket potatoes

Potatoes are also grown differently. They are planted in April. Did you know you can grow potatoes in a bucket? You don't even need a garden to do this. Ask if you can have an old plastic bucket. It should be big enough to hold at least 12 litres. Ask an adult to cut some holes in the base of the bucket. You should half fill the bucket with a mixture of soil and compost. Lay two sprouted seed potatoes on the soil.

Seed potatoes are not the same as the potatoes you eat for dinner. You can buy seed potatoes at the market, or from a garden centre, or perhaps you know a farmer who can give you some seed potatoes.

Cover your seed potatoes with 10 centimetres of soil, water the soil until it is damp, and put the bucket in a warm corner. Now you have to wait. The first green shoots should appear in about two weeks. They need to be covered over with more soil. Keep on covering the shoots as soon as they appear, and keep the soil damp.

When the soil has almost reached the top of the bucket, leave the potato plants to grow. They need plenty of nutrients, so you should fertilise them once a week. You could use diluted nettle tea or ask your parents whether they

Half fill a bucket with soil . . .

. . . and put in two seed potatoes.

Sprouted seed potatoes.

Flowering potato plants are very pretty.

have an organic fertiliser that can be added to water. Three grams of fertiliser should be mixed with one litre of water. As you will see, potatoes have very pretty little white flowers. They also develop small green fruit that look like green tomatoes. Take care that you don't eat them, as they are not tomatoes at all but very poisonous.

In about 10 weeks you can tip up the bucket. What a surprise! You will find about one and a half kilograms of potatoes attached to each potato plant. These potatoes can be eaten, skins and all. (After they have been cooked, of course!)

Trees don't look very interesting when you buy them.

Let's plant an apple tree

Planting a tree is hard work, and needs a strong adult. But there are things you can do to help, and at the same time you can learn more about trees. First of all you should go with your parents to the garden centre or tree nursery and have a good look around.

It is called a nursery, because it is a little like a nursery for human babies and young children. The baby trees and young trees are looked after and taught to grow the right way, just as young children have to learn to walk and talk. A nursery worker helps trees to grow the right way by cutting off certain branches. Nursery workers have to know a lot about how trees grow.

Trees ready to be sold in nurseries stand around in rows. They might be in pots, or growing in the ground, or their roots might be wrapped up in hessian. Apple trees are usually sold with their roots uncovered, since they are dug out of the ground only when you want to buy one. An apple tree doesn't look very interesting like this, with no leaves and spindly little twigs. It won't have any leaves because they will have fallen off, since it is usual to plant trees in autumn. Trees are usually sold when they are three or four years old.

With some help you can plant your own apple tree.

Your parents will need to dig a hole in the garden for the tree, perhaps even before you go to the nursery to buy it. The hole will be a bit bigger that the root ball. Usually some compost is mixed in with the soil in the hole and a stake is driven into the hole, not quite in the middle.

Now for the big moment! Check whether the ends of the roots need trimming. Now lay the handle of a leaf rake (or any garden tool) across the hole to show you how far down the tree should sit. The roots should all be below the handle and the stem above it. Once you have the tree at the right depth, you can hold it up straight while someone else shovels soil back into the hole. There shouldn't be any gaps, so pour in some water every once in a while to wash soil in between the roots. Once the hole has been filled up, firm the soil by treading on it gently. Now the tree needs a good watering, and needs to be tied to the stake. You see, its roots will take several months to grow into the soil, and in the meantime a strong wind could blow the tree over.

Next year you will have the pleasure of watching your tree as it blossoms and unfolds its leaves. You might even get an apple in the autumn!

55

Growing Different Plants Together

Plants are rather like people: some get on well with each other and some just don't like each other. Plants give off smells and their roots release certain substances into the soil, which another plant might or might not like. Plants in the wild choose their neighbours with these things in mind, so you should plan your garden so that plants are next to their friends. Look at the table carefully and you will see what plants can go into the same patch of garden together. Following these rules of nature will produce happier, healthier vegetables.

If you plant an early crop in April then you will harvest your crop in summer. And then you can plant something else! This is called rotation cropping and occurs in the wild too. After all, wild summer flowers (like poppies) don't bloom until after the spring flowers (like bluebells) have wilted.

Choosing which plants will grow happily beside each other also depends on the form of the leaves and the roots, the height of the plants and how quickly they grow. Late developers like growing next to early developers, plants with deep roots like being next to plants with shallow roots,

short, bushy plants like being next to tall, slim plants.

Most important of all are the plants' different tastes. As you know, some like plenty of nitrogen, others prefer phosphate. If you put the right plants together then they can share the nutrients in the soil, and each plant will take what it wants. But if, for example, all the plants like nitrogen, then they will quickly use up all the nitrogen in the soil.

You may wonder how farmers manage to grow whole fields of the same vegetable or other crop. They can do that only if they keep on fertilising the field; if a farmer grows the same crop in the same field, year after year, the soil will suffer. You too would be unhealthy if you ate only one kind of food. Growing the same crop every year is called monoculture. It is better for the soil if the farmer grows one crop this year and a different crop next year. This is called crop rotation, and you can read more about this later.

Here are a few suggestions as to what you can grow in spring, summer and autumn. Plants to be grown in spring ('early' crops) must be hardy, which means that they mustn't mind getting cold.

They must mature quickly too.

'Maturing' means growing to the full size and being ready to pick. Working out what to sow and when to sow it can be quite complicated, because there are early varieties and main crop varieties of the same fruits and vegetables. 'Main crop' varieties are sown in June and mature in August, so you see, you could be harvesting vegetables over several months.

Vegetables that are most suitable as early crops include spinach, radishes, all sorts of lettuce, carrots and cress.

Vegetables that take longer to grow are usually grown as main crops. They include cabbage, celery, onions, beans, beetroot and chicory.

Some vegetables can be grown over winter. They are called late or winter varieties. But growing them is really quite complicated, and probably best left to experienced gardeners.

When you are buying seeds, be sure to check that the variety of the vegetable is the one you want. This information should be on the seed packet, but ask a shop assistant if you're not sure. You probably want, for example, early crop radishes and main crop beans.

Companion planting: who gets on well with whom?

	Plant	Gets on well with:	Doesn't like being next to:
	beans	lettuce, cucumbers, tomatoes, potatoes, beetroot, savory	garlic, peas, leeks, onions
	peas	carrots, radishes, cucumbers, lettuce, kohlrabi, dill	beans, leek, onions, potatoes
	cucumber	beans, peas, onions, leeks, beetroot, lettuce, dill	radishes, tomatoes, potatoes
	potatoes	kohlrabi, spinach, beans, garlic, nasturtiums, peppermint	cucumbers, peas, tomatoes, beetroot
	garlic	carrots, cucumbers, beetroot, tomatoes	beans, peas, kohlrabi
	kohlrabi	beans, spinach, beetroot, leeks, lettuce, peas, potatoes	garlic
	carrots	onions, tomatoes, radishes, garlic, leek, peas, lettuce, dill	beetroot
	leeks	onions, carrots, tomatoes, lettuce, kohlrabi, camomile	beans, beetroot, peas
	radishes	lettuce, beans, spinach, tomatoes, kohlrabi, carrots, peas, cress	cucumbers
	beetroot	onions, kohlrabi, lettuce, garlic, cucumbers, dill	leeks, beans, spinach, potatoes
	lettuce	radishes, carrots, cucumbers, carrots, onion, tomatoes, beans, beetroot, leeks, kohlrabi, garlic	
	spinach	tomatoes, beans, radishes, kohlrabi, potatoes	beetroot
	tomatoes	carrots, beetroot, spinach, radishes, lettuce, leeks, kohlrabi, garlic	peas, cucumbers, potatoes
	onions	lettuce, carrots, beetroot, cucumber, dill, savory, camomile	peas, beans, kohlrabi

The herb garden

What's a vegetable patch without kitchen herbs? Some herbs can be grown amongst the vegetables, others need a patch of their own because they need a certain type of soil and have their own likes and dislikes. Dill gets on well with several types of vegetables. It will grow well next to peas, lettuce, carrots and onions. Parsley and tomatoes like each other's company, while savory likes beans and onions. Chives will grow almost everywhere.

Why don't you try growing camomile and peppermint? You can dry some of the leaves and make tea from them. What's more, they are attractive plants with pretty flowers. There are various kinds of camomile and peppermint, but you can make tea from only one kind. This is where the scientific name of plants comes in handy, as it tells you exactly which plant you want. To make camomile tea you need to buy the camomile plant called 'Matricaria chamomilla'. Peppermint tea is made from 'Mentha piperita'. You might have to go to a health food shop or a special herbalist's shop to buy them.

Camomile and peppermint can be grown amongst vegetables. Camomile particularly likes leek and onions, while peppermint likes kohlrabi and lettuce.

Many kitchen herbs come from Mediterranean countries, like Italy, and they still have the same habits and tastes as they did in their native land. They need plenty of sun, only a little water and usually only small quantities of nutrients. These herbs include marjoram, rosemary, lemon balm, sage, thyme and hyssop. They need a separate little patch of garden. Perhaps one of your parents would like to help you make a herb garden.

Camomile   Peppermint   Dill   Chives   Parsley   Savory

Nasturtiums

Marigolds

Tagetes

Well, it's up to you. You can grow vegetables, kitchen herbs, and herbs to make tea. How about a few flowers as well? Some flowers, for example marigolds and tagetes, like to grow next to vegetables. You can buy marigold and tagetes plants in spring at the market or at a garden centre. Nasturtiums also do well amongst vegetables and are easy to grow from seed. The seed is the size of a pea, and should be inserted about two centimetres into the soil in May. If you do want to grow flowers, be sure to leave enough room for them when you plant the vegetables.

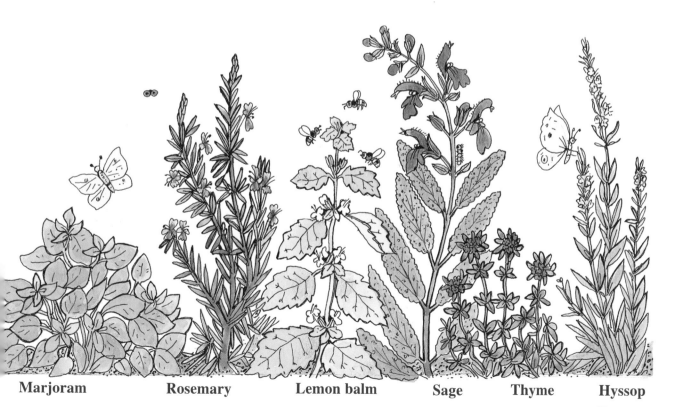

Marjoram   **Rosemary**   **Lemon balm**   **Sage**   **Thyme**   **Hyssop**

Crop rotation

By now you know that plants have different-sized appetites and make different demands on the soil. Very hungry plants are called heavy feeders. They include cucumber and kohlrabi. Medium feeders have a medium appetite: these include lettuce, beetroot, leeks, carrots, radishes, spinach, tomatoes and onions. Beans and peas are light feeders and don't eat much at all. Because they are legumes - remember, they are the plants that store nitrogen in nodules on their roots - they even put food back into the soil.

How does this affect your garden? Suppose you want to grow vegetables again next year, and perhaps the year after, too. Remember where in the bed you planted everything - perhaps you could keep the drawing you made when you were planning your garden. Next year you should plant medium feeders where the heavy feeders were growing this year. This means, for example, that next year you should plant spinach where cucumber are growing now. The year after, you should plant a light feeder, for example beans. And the year after that, you can plant a heavy feeder again. This means that you should grow a heavy feeder in the same place only every four years.

Farmers used to choose their crops according to this rule of crop rotation. That was up until about a hundred years ago, when farms were smaller and there were fewer people. Every fourth year the farmers would give a field a rest by not growing anything on it. This is called letting it lie fallow. All sorts of wild plants would start to grow on the fallow field: clover, vetch, lupins and others. Some of these wild plants, the legumes, would add nitrogen to the soil, others had the task of breaking up the soil with their long roots. In spring the farmer would take his horse and plough to the fallow field and plough all the wild plants under. This is green manuring on a large scale. If the farmer wanted to add more nutrients to the soil, he would scatter a cartload of manure over the field before he ploughed it.

You might find seeds for wild field plants in a garden centre. Sometimes they are sold separately (like clover) and sometimes you can buy packets of mixed seeds. Growing a crop for green manuring needn't take very long. If you sow the green manure crop in March you can cut the crop at the beginning of May. Leave the stalks and everything lying on top of the soil. Rake them off in mid-May and put them on the compost heap. Then dig the ground and prepare it for main crop varieties of vegetables and summer flowers. Alternatively you could sow a crop for green manuring in autumn and leave it in the ground until spring.

Growing tomatoes from seed takes a long time. It is a lot easier to buy tomato plants, which are

Cucumbers and kohlrabi are heavy eaters, the vegetables in the middle are medium feeders . . .

. . . and beans and peas have small appetites.

available in mid-May. They don't like cold, so put them in a warm, sunny spot. Dig a hole for each plant and then drive a cane into the hole. Later on you can tie the tomato plants to the cane. Tie the end to the cane as soon as it has grown a few centimetres. The tomato plant will grow quite quickly, so keep an eye on it and tie any new growth to the stake.

At some stage you will discover the first yellow flowers. You will need to remove some clusters of flowers if you want big tomatoes. Leave four clusters of flowers on each plant. You also need to break off the side shoots which grow out of the stem where the leaves join on, because otherwise the plant will put too much energy into producing leaves. You want it to produce nice, juicy tomatoes! You can leave the broken-off flowers and shoots on the ground around the plant, as it will like this.

The tomato plants will keep on producing flowers. Once you have started to pick tomatoes you can leave more flowers on the plant and then you will get more tomatoes later. You can pick tomatoes before they are quite red, and they will ripen indoors on a plate.

Be sure to water your tomato plants regularly. Tomato plants are thirsty and like the soil around them to be damp all the time.

Strawberries have their own

Tomatoes need a stake and need to be watered regularly.

special requirements too. If you want strawberries in June then you will have to start preparing the bed almost a year earlier, in August! After an adult has forked over the soil, hoe in some compost and organic fertiliser.

Plant the strawberry plants 25 centimetres apart and cover the soil with a layer of garden waste, bark mulch or straw. Now you can leave your strawberries over the winter. Next spring you rake away any bigger pieces of the mulch (you can read more about mulches on the next page) and hoe the ground. Now cover the soil with fresh straw. This has two uses. It keeps the soil damp and

Tomatoes and strawberries have their own likes and dislikes.

Straw keeps the soil damp and also stops the fruit rotting.

helps prevent weeds from growing. It also keeps your delicious strawberries off the ground and stops them rotting.

After you have harvested your strawberries fertilise the strawberry bed with some diluted nettle tea, then prepare the bed for winter as you did last year. All through summer the soil should be kept damp - strawberries are thirsty. The same strawberry plants will produce plenty of strawberries for three or four years. After that you should dig them out and replace them with new plants.

Strawberry plants send out long shoots (runners) which develop into new plants. A few of these new plants can be left to grow, especially those new plants which are growing from a 'parent' plant that produces lots of strawberries. Cut the other new plants off, or your strawberry bed will soon get very crowded.

Care

Now you know the most important things about sowing, planting out, companion planting, and crop rotation. That's not all there is to gardening, of course. The weather helps to decide what else you have to do. Plants, like you, enjoy sunshine - but not all the time. They also need rain, and if it doesn't rain then you have to water them.

Watering is usually done early in the morning or in the early evening. If you need to rush in the morning to get to school on time then it is probably a good idea to water your garden in the evening instead.

Gardeners usually avoid watering in the late morning or early afternoon because the heat makes the wet soil dry quickly and turn hard. What's more, the hot midday sun could scorch wet leaves, because drops of water act like mini magnifying glasses, and it is difficult not to get water on the leaves when watering.

Have you ever held a magnifying glass over a piece of paper outside in the hot sun? The magnifying glass magnifies the sun and the paper starts to burn. Drops of water have the same effect on leaves. The sun magnifies the drops of water and burns

It is best to water your garden in the evening or the morning when there is no danger of your plants being scorched.

the leaves, making ugly brown marks and weakening the plant.

While plants use some of the water in the soil, some water is wasted by evaporating through the soil. You can prevent this evaporation by spreading a mulch on the soil. A mulch is a layer of material, usually plant waste, covering the soil.

Have a look at the ground in a forest or woods, or under bushes growing wild. You probably won't see much soil. Instead it will be covered with small plants, dead leaves, moss and tangled

growth, forming a natural mulch. The soil underneath all this is damp, since the moisture cannot evaporate quickly.

You can make a mulch for your garden with grass cuttings. Spread it loosely over the soil, remembering that the soil must be able to breathe. You could also use straw, or garden waste cut up small and mixed with a little compost.

Flowers can be mulched with bark chips or bark mulch, which is a waste product of saw mills. When trees are sawn up into planks of wood the bark isn't used, and some of this waste bark is chopped finely and made into bark chips. Bark mulch is made of even more finely chopped bark. You can buy bark chips and bark mulch at garden centres.

Some people spread peat over the soil, but this does little good.

Peat adds no nutrients to the soil. However, some flowering bushes (such as rhododendrons, azaleas and heaths) like peat because it makes the soil acidic. Vegetables don't want an acidic soil and in general they have no use for peat.

You might be wondering what peat is. It comes from moorland. Moors are biotopes and provide a

Bark mulch.

Straw mulch.

home to many plants and animals that cannot live anywhere else. Peat performs the same functions in a moor as soil does in your garden. Peat is cut out of moors and taken away to lie around in gardens. Now although peat isn't very useful in a garden, it is very important on a moor, so important that the plants and animals living there die if the peat is taken away.

Peat takes thousands of years to grow, so it is much more sensible to use compost or plant waste on your garden - after all, it only takes a year or so to produce new soil on a compost heap.

Spread a mulch between rows of seeds and seedlings. The soil

will stay damp for far longer, and you won't have to water and weed the garden so often.

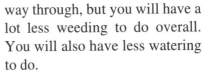

A gardener has to water the garden . . .

. . . hoe it . . .

. . . mulch it . . .

Mulching helps prevent weeds. Although weeds do have their uses (for example, they provide food for animals), they can be a nuisance in the garden, particularly in a vegetable patch, because they have appetites like any plant and can take nutrients away from your vegetables. You should pull them out as soon as they appear. Weeds can grow unbelievably quickly: you might weed your patch one day, and three days later you will need to do it again.

Weeds will find it difficult to grow if you cover the soil with a layer of mulch. It's not easy for a little weed to fight its way through a layer of grass clippings (or whatever you use). Very stubborn weeds will eventually make their way through, but you will have a lot less weeding to do overall. You will also have less watering to do.

Hoeing is another task you have to do less often if you mulch. Soil without mulch dries out more quickly and often forms a hard crust on the surface, which might be one or two centimetres thick. The sun, wind and rain help to make this crust. Sometimes the crust is so hard that water cannot soak into the soil and then the plants suffer. The plant will be hungry as well as thirsty, because the plant needs water to transport nutrients around the plant.

You need to hoe in between the rows at least twice a week, just to scratch open the hard surface.

If you have mulched your garden then the sun, wind and rain can't reach the surface to make it crusty and the soil will remain loose for much longer.

Mulch gradually disappears, and you will have to add more after a few weeks. Hoe the soil thoroughly before you spread over the fresh mulch.

Fertilising is also part of a gardener's work. How often you need to fertilise depends on the quality of the soil and the type of mulch you use. Healthy, rich soil needs less fertiliser than a sandy or gravelly soil. Mulching with compost and garden waste means that you need less fertiliser, and if the soil is already healthy then you won't need to fertilise at all.

... fertilise it ...

... and loosen the soil.

If you're using straw mulch, which doesn't contain many nutrients, use diluted nettle tea or an organic fertiliser as well.

A garden shredder works like a large coffee grinder: you put the garden waste in at the top, and shredded waste comes out the bottom, ready to use as mulch.

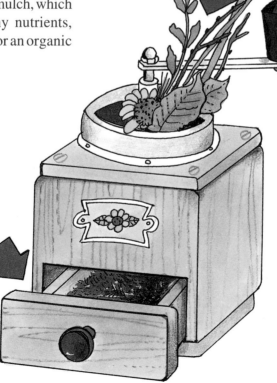

The normal time to fertilise the garden is when you have harvested the first vegetables. The first crop uses up many of the nutrients in the soil, so you need to replace them before you can sow or plant the next crop.

So apart from sowing and planting, a gardener must mulch, water, weed, hoe and fertilise. And when the growing season has finished and you have harvested the last vegetables, the garden has to be prepared for its winter rest. Cut off the rest of the plants and leave them lying on the soil. Maybe your parents have a shredding machine. A garden shredding machine, or shredder, is big enough to take pieces of garden waste. Cutting blades inside the machine cut up the waste so that it comes out below in small chips or shreds.

Shredded plant waste is the best winter blanket you can put on a garden. Spread a little compost over the soil first, then a thick layer of garden waste, shredded or just cut up a bit. Now you can leave your garden for the winter. By spring much of the garden waste will have disappeared, and you can rake up what remains and put it on the compost heap. A new gardening year can begin.

Protecting Plants

Now for a complicated chapter. Plants sometimes get sick. Here, too, they are a bit like people: if they are well fed then they don't get sick so easily. So the better the soil in your patch of garden, the fewer problems you will have with sick and diseased plants. Unfortunately it is unlikely that your plants will have no problems at all, however healthy they are.

Some gardeners use chemical 'medicines' at the first sign of trouble. These are often very poisonous. There are old household cures for plants, just as there are for people. You can make some of these yourself, as long as an adult is there to help.

You already know how to make nettle tea. Nettle tea is not only a good fertiliser, it also protects plants from mildew and spider mites. Mildew is the powdery white film you sometimes find on the leaves of roses and cucumbers. Spider mites are tiny insects that suck the leaves.

You can make a similar tea with field horsetail. You probably won't find this in a garden. It can sometimes be bought dried from special herbalist's shops, or try a big health food shop that sells environmentally friendly goods as well as food. You need to boil 150 grams of dried field horsetail in 10 litres of water. Be sure to ask an adult to help you, as 10 litres of boiling water is very heavy and very dangerous. Now move the pot outside and leave it for a few days. Dilute this field horsetail tea one part to five: this means that you measure out for example 100 millilitres of field horsetail tea and add 500 millilitres of fresh water. Spraying this over your plants helps them to fight off illness and kills aphids.

Kitchen waste can be used to make medicine for your plants. Collect onion and garlic skins until you have 500 grams. (That's a lot of skins! Perhaps you could start collecting them in winter.) Put them in a bucket with 10 litres of

field horsetail

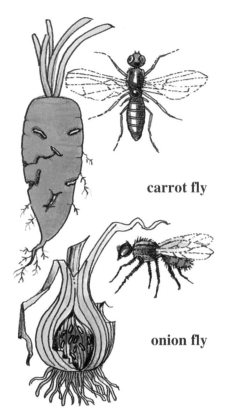

carrot fly

onion fly

If you plant your carrots and onions next to each other, neither the carrot fly nor the onion fly will attack them - and you won't need to use poisonous sprays.

water, cover the bucket, and leave it outside for several days. Dilute this tea one part to ten and use it to protect strawberries against insect damage and against aphids.

Snails can be a real problem in a garden. Snails might crawl very slowly, but they eat very quickly, and they take no time at all to eat great holes in a lettuce leaf. There are several methods of killing them, using poisons or traps. None of these methods is very nice for the snails, and it is easier for you and kinder to the snails if you simply stop them going on to your garden. You can buy snail 'fences' from garden centres. This is plastic tape which you lay around the edges of your garden. Snails can't crawl over this tape and so they can't eat your vegetable seedlings.

It is easy to avoid trouble from the carrot fly and the onion fly. Sow or plant onions and carrots together: one carrot, then one onion, then one carrot, and so on. You see, carrot flies can't stand the smell of onions, and onion flies can't stand the smell of carrots. So they both leave! If you remember this trick when planning your garden you will save yourself a lot of work, and you won't need to use poisonous sprays.

Natural and organic methods of protecting plants work with both flowers and vegetables. Garlic is good for people and for the garden too. It helps to protect plants from mildew and for this reason many gardeners grow garlic amongst roses.

A few pages back you read that it is a good idea to plant a few flowers in a vegetable patch. A useful flower to plant is tagetes, which has pretty orange flowers. It looks nice and at the same time protects your vegetables from eelworm. Eelworm are small worms in the soil that like to eat the roots of vegetables. Tagetes roots contain a natural chemical that acts like a magnet to eelworm. They rush over to the tagetes roots and eat some, but this chemical is actually poisonous to eelworm and will kill them.

Another way of getting rid of eelworm is to plant marigolds or camomile. Eelworm don't like the smell of marigolds or camomile. A single camomile plant is enough to keep a vegetable patch free of eel-worm.

Ants can be a real nuisance, especially when they decide to snack on your strawberries. Planting lavender and marjoram between the rows will put the ants right off and they will search for food elsewhere.

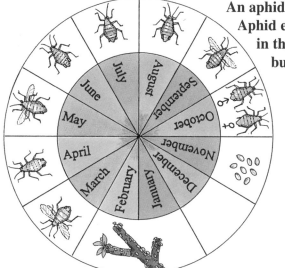

An aphid's life is complicated. Aphid eggs spend the winter in the shelter of trees and bushes. Female aphids emerge in March. They don't lay eggs or mate, but bear young females. The males are born in autumn. They mate with the females. These females lay eggs which lie dormant over the winter.

There are pests which specialise in one sort of plant. The black bean aphid, for example, loves beans. But it prefers nasturtiums, and you can plant nasturtiums near beans as a sort of trap. The black bean aphids will go and feast on the nasturtiums and leave the beans alone. As soon as a lot of bean aphids have collected on the nasturtiums you should pull them out and sow some more nasturtiums seeds. You will soon have fresh nasturtiums to attract the bean aphids away from the beans. By the way, the infested nasturtiums you pull out should be thrown away with the rubbish, and not put on the compost heap. In general, you should not put sick or infested plants on the compost heap.

You can catch the bean aphid with nasturtiums, but remember to throw the infested plants into the rubbish bin, not on the compost heap.

You can probably guess what plant the pea moth likes. The caterpillar of a pea moth is small, greenish-yellow and eats its way through a pod of peas in no time. But if carrots, tomatoes or marigolds are growing nearby then the pea moth will lose its appetite.

Cabbage-white butterflies can do a lot of damage. They love the leaves of all sorts of cabbage and its relatives. Fortunately there are several plants which will send the cabbage-white butterfly packing: Dill needs to be growing close by, leeks and tomatoes should be within smelling distance, and rosemary can be a short distance away.

The strawberry blossom weevil can ruin a whole crop of strawberries. This little beetle spends the winter in your cosy strawberry bed. In spring it crawls up into the strawberry flowers, where it lays its eggs, and as a result no strawberries develop. You can get rid of this pest by laying a few fern fronds between the rows. Ferns grow wild in the woods, and, if you ask first, the owner might let you cut a few fronds there.

The cutworm will eat just about any fruit or vegetable it finds: lettuce, cabbage, carrots, radishes, strawberries, spinach, and others besides. Cutworms usually have their feasts at night. During the day they wriggle back into the soil. They too can be chased away

The caterpillar of the cabbage-white butterfly.

with fern fronds.

These are all natural methods of protecting plants. There are also so-called mechanical methods, often used to protect fruit trees. You might have seen a fruit tree with a sticky band wrapped around its trunk, about one metre from the ground. Many insects will try to crawl up the trunks of trees in autumn in order to lay their eggs somewhere high up in the tree. The winter moth is one of these. In spring the eggs hatch and the little caterpillars feast on the fresh, tender young leaves and blossoms. They can be so greedy that they eat all the leaves and blossoms, and then, of course, there won't be any fruit. But a sticky band wrapped around the tree stops the female winter moth crawling up and laying her eggs.

When you bite into a cherry, the last thing you want to find is a little worm. The cherry fruit fly is to blame.

Larvae of a pea moth.

Cutworm.

treat mildew. Neither chrysanthemums nor soya beans are poisonous in their natural form. The sprays are made by concentrating a chemical found in the plant.

Bean aphid.

Caterpillar of a winter moth.

This fly is about the same size as an ordinary house-fly and lays its eggs on cherries. Once the eggs hatch, the worms crawl into the cherries and have a wonderful time. Fortunately there is a way of stopping this. Cherry fruit flies love the colour yellow, so if you hang circles of sticky yellow paper in the tree in May, the cherry fruit fly will land on the yellow paper and stay stuck.

You're bound to be curious about chemical methods of protecting plants. You can buy sprays from garden centres which will get rid of many of these pests. They are very effective, but they can harm many other insects too, including insects that are useful to us. Sprays made from plants are not poisonous to all insects. For example, sprays made from chrysanthemums - those pretty flowers that bloom late in summer - kill many harmful insects but do not hurt bees. Soya bean plants are also used to make a spray to

You can use sticky yellow paper circles to catch cherry fruit flies, because they love the colour yellow.

Helpful Friends

Remember Wiggle the worm and his helpful friends? And the micro-organisms in the soil? A gardener will find even more helpful friends among the insects in a garden, including some that help to control pests. This is called biological pest control.

Spiders eat many insects that we regard as pests, such as flies, midges and aphids. Be sure to leave any spiders' nests you find. You needn't worry that you will be taken over by spiders, as they too are eaten, for example by the great tit and the parasite wasp. There are about 650 varieties of spiders in the British Isles. There is no need to be afraid of our spiders. Although they are all poisonous, this is only to the insects they catch, and they are completely harmless to humans.

The spider mite is a very small, and very annoying, type of spider, at least for a gardener. They are also called red spiders. These tiny red creatures sit under the leaves of tomatoes, cucumbers, beans and fruit trees. They suck sap from the leaves and can cause a lot of harm over time.

Fortunately for us, the red spider mite has an enemy, another type of spider mite called the predatory mite. Predatory mites like nothing more than feasting on red spiders. So if gardeners discover red spiders in a greenhouse they can buy some predatory mites - yes, you can buy them - and let them loose in the greenhouse. Once the predatory mites have eaten up all the red spiders they will die.

There are plenty of other useful insects. The ladybird, which Americans call ladybug, is one. Ladybirds not only look pretty, they also do a splendid job eating aphids. The ladybirds you're probably familiar with - the red ones with black spots - are just one member of a large family.

They have about 70 types of relations, some with yellow or black patterns. Most types of ladybirds eat aphids, but some also eat red spiders or mildew fungus.

As their name suggests, lace-wings are pretty, delicate insects.

Perhaps you have learnt in science at school that insects take on different forms at different stages of their life. An insect starts life as an egg, from which it develops into a larva, worm, or caterpillar. Some insects then spin themselves into a cocoon.

When the adult insect emerges it looks quite different. It might have become a butterfly or some other winged insect. This adult insect has to lay eggs so that the cycle can start again.

Predatory mites eat red spiders.

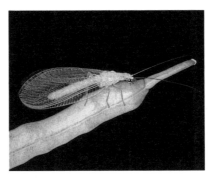

A lace-wing larva will gobble up hundreds of aphids.

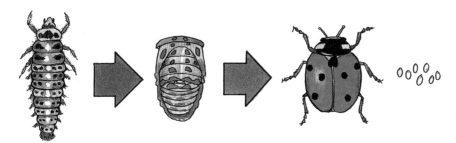

Lace-wings were larvae before they developed into flying insects, and as larvae they help the gardener a great deal. A single tiny lace-wing larva eats several hundred aphids in two or three weeks!

If you ever discover a lace-wing in your garden, take a close look. A golden strip runs along its long, narrow, green body. Its eyes gleam golden, and a network of fine, green veins covers the otherwise transparent wings. The lace-wing is a very attractive insect.

You have a friend in the hover-fly as well. Hover-flies look rather like wasps, which are not so nice to have around. Unlike wasps, hover-flies are completely harmless. They are easy to distinguish them from wasps, since the hover-fly sometimes hovers in the air and then suddenly flies on. Wasps cannot do this.

As larvae, hover-flies munch their way through a lot of aphids.

They live for only two weeks, but in this time each one gets through 600 to 700 aphids.

Many types of beetle find plenty to eat in the garden. The big black ground beetle feeds on snails. Other beetles feed on worms and insect eggs lying near the soil surface. That includes the eggs of the cabbage fly - a very greedy insect that can wipe out your cabbage crop. Some beetles crawl up fruit trees and keep order up there.

Some sorts of beetles are not useful. Cockchafers and their larvae - grubs - are quite a nuisance. The grubs live in the soil and eat roots, while the cockchafers eat holes in leaves and stalks. However, they do provide tasty treats for other animals. Partridges and pheasants pick the grubs out of the soil, and hedgehogs and moles gobble them up too. Several types of birds - crows, for example - are very fond of the adult cockchafer.

Adult ladybirds (or ladybugs) are pretty, but they didn't always look like that. The egg develops into a larva that feeds on aphids. Later on the larva forms itself into a cocoon, from which, eventually, the ladybird emerges and lays her eggs.

A single ladybird can eat up to 150 aphids a day. This makes it a very useful friend indeed.

trees. A few days later the pots are full of earwigs. They sleep in the pots during the day and go out aphid-hunting at night.

Even if your garden is on your balcony you can try using these biological methods of pest control. Even earwigs will make it to at least the second floor. But if one of your flower plants becomes infested with insects then it is better to dig it up and throw it away, because otherwise all your plants might become infested.

There are many other insects that belong in your garden. If you look at the overall picture of life in a garden, you will see that everything has its place, even if it is just to provide dinner for another animal. So don't squash every caterpillar, beetle or larva you see, and let the flies fly away.

There are two more visitors to your garden that should be mentioned. They don't eat any aphids, but they are nevertheless very important for your garden: honey bees and bumblebees. They fly tirelessly from flower to flower in search of nectar, and carry pollen from one plant to the next.

A bee searching for nectar.

A plant pot stuffed with wood shavings makes a good earwig hide-away.

Earwigs are another insect that some people dislike. They are, of course, quite harmless, and won't crawl into your ear and bite you, or sting you either. Earwigs will occasionally munch on tender green buds and shoots, but they more than make up for this by eating aphids. Earwigs like to go aphid-hunting at night. They eat so many aphids that even professional gardeners try to attract earwigs into gardens. Fruit growers fill plant pots with wood shavings, seal the top, and hang the pots upside down under fruit

A bumblebee feeding.

you a nasty sting, there are other types that are quite peaceful and help you to control pests. The parasitic wasp is one of these. It has its own method of attack: it lays its eggs in the larvae, pupae or eggs of other insects. The parasitic wasp larvae develop and eat their 'home' from within.

Have you heard of bed bugs? They are little bugs that live in old beds and like human blood. They have very useful relations that feed on red spiders, aphids and the larvae of midges.

All these small insects belong in the garden too. And last but not least, let's not forget the billions of organisms living in the soil.

The fine grains of pollen stick to their hairy bodies and are then picked up by the sticky stigmas of other flowers. You will have already read about this in the chapter about seeds. If there were no honey bees or bumblebees then there wouldn't be such delicious things as apples, pears, cherries, plums, tomatoes and cucumbers, and no honey either.

Both honey bees and bumblebees have a difficult life. Sprays used against unwanted insects (insecticides) cannot tell the difference between useful insects, like bees, and pests, like aphids. There are some sprays that are not harmful to bees, but you won't need them if a good

variety of plants and animals (including insects) live in your garden.

You can think of it like a set of scales. The useful plants are on one side and the pests are on the other. If the right numbers of both are around, then the scales will balance evenly. This is called the balance of nature. Nature will create this balance if given the opportunity, so it is best not to interfere.

You've read about spiders, earwigs, ladybirds, beetles, hover-flies, lace-wings, honey bees and bumblebees. Wasps, which belong to the same family as honey bees, bumblebees and ants, are not just pests. While some wasps can give

Parasitic wasps.

Butterflies

What would a summer meadow be without butterflies? You're certain to have seen a butterfly. They come in all sorts of colours. Some are yellow with small black spots, others are brown with blue 'eyes' on the wings, others are black with red and white stripes on the edges of their wings.

There used to be many more butterflies than there are today. This is partly because there used to be more wild plants around. Butterflies tend to like exactly those plants that people generally think of as weeds and pull out.

Almost all butterflies are vegetarians, which means that they feed only on plants. Many are very fussy and stubborn about what they want to eat. This can cause problems for them. Butterflies, like most other insects, spend a large part of their life as caterpillars. And caterpillars are by nature hungry. The caterpillar of the cabbage-white butterfly is a good example. It can munch its way through a lot of cabbage leaves, much to the annoyance of gardeners! Once the caterpillar of the cabbage-white butterfly becomes a butterfly, it just sips delicately at nectar and dew.

Some people living in the countryside still keep cabbage-white butterfly caterpillars under control by letting their hens loose in the cabbage patch. The hens have a wonderful time feasting on all sorts of caterpillars and worms. Hens are very handy animals to have around in a garden, and some fruit growers keep hens to help control insects. The hens run around under the trees and gobble

Fox tail.

Brimstone.

Lycaenid (Common Blue).

up insects that have fallen from the trees or that are lying about as pupae. Hens have very large appetites!

A few more words about butterflies. Some are now endangered and may soon become extinct if we don't help them.

You have already read about how useful nettles can be. You can make a good fertiliser from them, nettle tea. Nettles are also useful for some butterflies including the Peacock butterfly, the Small Tortoiseshell butterfly, the Red Admiral, and others. The female butterflies lay their eggs on nettles because their caterpillars eat almost nothing but nettle leaves.

Many butterflies need certain plants in order to be able to survive: the Lycaenid or Common Blue needs clover and vetch, the Painted Lady likes thistles best, and the Copper butterfly eats almost entirely sorrel and other bog plants.

Butterfly caterpillars won't have a lot of respect for your plants. The caterpillar of the Fritillary, a big light-brown butterfly with a pretty dark pattern, prefers violets and strawberries. The White Admiral needs gorse if its pupae are to turn into caterpillars and then butterflies. The attractive Swallow-tail butterfly makes its home in dill and fennel. And the Yellow Brimstone likes black alder and buckthorn leaves.

Most butterflies live and feed in meadows. Unfortunately there just aren't enough real meadows left now. Modern farm meadows tend to contain nothing much but grass, which is good for cows but useless for butterflies. A traditional meadow might have around 50 different types of plants growing in it, and about 40 different types of butterflies would live there. A farm field, however, will provide a home for only a few types of butterflies, which is a pity.

You can do something to help butterflies survive. If you find nettles growing in a corner of the garden, leave them to grow.

Perhaps you could talk with your parents about butterflies. You could suggest growing a butterfly meadow instead of lawn. This is quite easy to do, as garden centres now sell packets of mixed seed that will produce a meadow with lots of the plants butterflies like. A meadow has another advantage over a lawn: it needn't be cut every week in summer. A meadow should be cut only once or twice a year. And one more thing: don't squash caterpillars, because they might be butterfly caterpillars.

![Fritillary]

Fritillary.

Map butterfly (extinct in this country).

Birds

You will never be short of company while you are gardening if you plan your garden with birds in mind. Birds, like butterflies, need certain plants in order to survive. If you want to attract birds to your garden then you will have to provide them with these plants.

Birds enjoy feeding on seeds and sweet fruits, but they also like caterpillars, larvae, flies and all sorts of other insects. This helps to keep the balance of nature in your garden. The more birds that visit your garden, the less trouble you will have with insect pests.

Spring is an especially busy time for adult birds. They spend most of the day flying to and fro finding food for their young back in the nest, because baby birds are always hungry.

Perhaps you might have wondered whether gardening would be easier if there were no insects at all, except perhaps for bees. But if there were no insects, then most birds would starve and die. Then there would be no dawn chorus, no blackbirds hopping around on the lawn, no larksong.

Birds need a little help from us if we want them to feel at home in a garden. Providing them with nesting boxes is one way of doing this.

How many different types of bird do you know? You might not see all the birds listed here in your garden, but keep an eye open when you are out walking in the countryside.

The bluetit, the great tit and the coal-tit are frequent visitors to gardens. Their favourite nesting place is in hollow tree trunks, but they will take to a nesting box if it is the right shape and has the right sized entrance. The entrance shouldn't be too big, otherwise bigger birds (such as magpies) or squirrels or cats will be able to reach the eggs or the young birds.

Goldfinch.

Bluetit.

Greenfinch.

Blackbird.

Bullfinch.

In winter they will enjoy picking at a seed ball, especially if you hang it in the branches of a tree. In summer it needs huge quantities of caterpillars to feed its young.

Greenfinches make a great deal of noise and flap their wings about if they find a feeding table nicely laid out with bird food. They build their nests high up in trees and so won't be attracted to a nesting box lower down. They too feed their young with insects, but they prefer seeds. Plants that provide seeds include grasses, many shrubs, roses and common alder.

Blackbirds enjoy eating - and that's putting it kindly! You will often see them hopping about on the ground looking for worms.

There are plenty of worms in good healthy soil, so you needn't worry that the blackbirds will eat them all. In summer they move on to your raspberries, blackcurrants and other berries. You could try to protect your fruit by spreading big nets across beds and over trees, as professional fruit growers do.

Another bird attracted to fruit is the starling, but starlings do also help the gardener by eating a great many insects or larvae, particularly those of the crane-fly, the 'leatherjacket'. Like tits,

Starling.

starlings prefer nesting in tree hollows, but will also use nesting boxes, given the chance. Vast numbers of them migrate to roosts near major cities in the autumn, where it is slightly warmer in winter and there is more to eat.

You have probably seen the male bullfinch with its black cap and bright pink breast feathers. The bullfinch needs an area of thick bush or scrub to feel at home and to build a nest, and they will totally ignore nesting boxes. There might be a rather untidy corner at the back of your garden that would suit a bullfinch.

The bullfinch's favourite food is seed and also the buds of some fruit trees. In summer, they catch lots of insects to feed their young.

Songthrush.

Young people are usually curious, which is a very good thing. How else would you learn anything? But sometimes you have to learn to control your curiosity in a garden, and this is certainly the case with birds. In springtime birds need to be left in peace. If people come too close to a bird's territory, trying to find its nest, then they will disturb the bird and it might fly away. It might completely abandon its nest, even if there are eggs or young in it. No amount of peeping and chirping by the chicks will bring the parents back.

Robins, like bullfinches, prefer to nest in thick bushes. They build their nests in hollows in the ground between roots. (A surprising number of birds are ground nesting). Robins feed on insects during the summer and berries in winter. The berries robins eat are those growing on shrubs which we cannot eat.

If you want to plan your garden so as to attract birds, you should remember that British birds like the berries of plants native to the British Isles, and berries of 'exotic' plants - that is, plants which have been brought to Britain from another country - might not agree with them. If a shrub has no berries, then it won't provide any food at all.

You may be lucky enough to see a redstart, which can be recognised by its red tail-feathers. The redstart feeds almost entirely on insects. This tiny bird, smaller than a sparrow, will fly all the way to Africa for the winter but rarely rests in this country! Swallows are another type of bird that travels immense distances.

Redstart.

They spend our winter months in Southern Africa, south of the Sahara desert. Their return to us early in the year is a sure sign that spring is coming. Swallows commonly build nests under eaves in garages and warehouses. These nests are made of a mixture of mud, plant fibres and feathers. Swallows will sometimes nest in special man-made nests fixed up under the eaves.

Swallows are experts at manoeuvering themselves about in the air as they fly after insects. They like flying insects only, and they catch them while they are on the wing. You might have seen a swallow diving through the air, then suddenly darting off to one side. What a lot of work for one insect!

A swallow's nest.

Robin.

Sparrow.

Magpie.

The song thrush can be heard most often in the evening as it sits high up in a tree or on a television aerial, singing its lovely song. It finds its food, worms and larvae, in the ground. The song thrush finds snails a particular delicacy. Unfortunately it also likes a quick snack of fruit. Song thrushes always build their own nests, and nest in trees and bushes.

The cheeky little sparrow can be found everywhere. It will eat just about anything: insects, seeds, tender buds and sweet fruit. Sparrows have spread all over the world and like to live near people. Sparrows build their nests in tree hollows, holes in walls and nesting boxes.

There is one bird that you won't want to see in your garden, and that is the magpie. It does eat worms, larvae, snails and spiders, but it also plunders the nests of smaller birds and eats their eggs and the young birds. We might find this cruel, but it does have a purpose and helps to keep the balance of nature. You see, while millions of birds are born each spring, there just isn't enough food to feed all these birds, so some of them have to die. Nature arranges for some birds to be eaten by other birds. After all, the magpies have to eat too.

If people complain that there are now fewer birds than there used to be, this isn't the magpie's or any other bird's fault. Nor is the grey squirrel or your neighbour's cat to blame. There are fewer birds because people have destroyed their food, with poisonous sprays that kill insects, and their homes, by 'tidying up' the landscape and cutting down trees. Birds need hedges and untidy old bushes and trees.

Hedgehog and Co.

So far you have read about worms, beetles, spiders, snails, butterflies and birds. Other animals, like hedgehogs, live in your garden too. If you hear something rustling and snuffling about in the undergrowth, it might just be a hedgehog together with its family. These funny little creatures feed on snails, slugs, spiders and beetles. They will also plunder eggs from the nests of ground-nesting birds.

You won't often see this prickly chap during the day. Hedgehogs don't usually become active until the evening, and then they spend the night searching for food. This timetable isn't without its problems. Hedgehogs are often run over at night as they scurry across the road. Hedgehogs play an important part in keeping the balance of nature and we should do all we can to help them. Some people think they can help hedgehogs by bringing them inside and keeping them in a box, but this actually harms them. Hedgehogs like to hide in undergrowth under dead leaves and sleep all day. It is difficult for them to do this if a garden is too tidy, or if it is very noisy. Hedgehogs don't particularly like dogs barking and sniffing at them either.

If you find a hedgehog in your garden then you should leave it in peace. Do not lay out saucers of milk for it as milk will make it ill, but they will enjoy a saucer of water, or some fresh dog food.

The mole is another animal that isn't very welcome in many gardens. Although they are very useful little creatures, feeding largely on insect pests that live in the ground and eat roots, they unfortunately make themselves unpopular in some gardens by tunnelling underground and popping up for air in the middle of lawns and flower-beds, creating mole hills - bare mounds of dug-up earth - where they emerge. This can be a real problem, even though it is quite easy to smooth over the molehill with a rake.

Mice also live outside in gardens, and as long as there are only a few there is no need to think of them as a nuisance. Nor is there any reason to be afraid of them either, as they are quite harmless. Shrews look similar to mice but are actually related to moles. Like the mole they eat insect pests, and should be welcomed in any garden. Some people kill them, mistaking them for mice.

The common toad will also help to protect your plants from insects. You may not find a toad in your garden unless there is a pond nearby as they need water to lay their eggs in, but otherwise they live on dry land. Snails are the greatest delicacy in the world to a toad, and it spends most of the night hunting them. Toads hide under pieces of wood, leaves and stones during the day. Toads are

Mole.

A hedgehog in a house.

also useful to a gardener, though some, like lizards, are rarely seen in gardens.

Some people don't like grass snakes. They are, however, not at all slimy, never attack people, and are completely harmless. What they do like is insects, and plenty of them. With so many animal helpers you really don't need poisonous sprays. Your garden can become a mini paradise for them all. Sometimes it is difficult to achieve a balance of nature, and a lot depends upon what your neighbours do. Insects and other animals cross from one garden to the next, and if your neighbours use poisonous sprays then 'your' insects and animals will be affected too.

Here you can see the army of animal helpers a gardener can rely on to catch insect pests.

The Garden in Winter

At the end of the growing season plants and many animals prepare for their winter rest. (Some animals hibernate in winter, which means they sleep for long periods.) Trees and shrubs lose their leaves, which fall on to the ground around them to keep the roots warm and to provide nutrients for next year's growth.

Annual flowers (flowers that live for only one season) die. So that they will not die out completely they have produced seeds, which they now let fall to the ground. In spring these seeds will sprout and grow into new flowers. The perennial plants (the plants that live for more than a year) wilt but their roots are still alive and will send up new shoots next year. You can help your garden to prepare for its winter rest. Harvest the last of your vegetables and then pull up the plants. Remember to leave the nitrogen-rich roots of the beans and peas (the legumes) in the soil. Just cut off the stalks and vines. Spread a little compost over the soil and cover it with the cut-off stalks and other waste that you have just removed. This will provide a blanket for the soil and let it recover from the hard work of the growing season. By spring it will have gathered strength.

A hedgehog will feel snug and cosy over the winter in a make-shift home like this.

Feeding stations need to be kept clean.

A silo feeder keeps feed dry.

Plants native to Britain will not need to be protected from the cold because they are used to our climate. They will survive the winter as long as the earth around them is covered with dead leaves or similar material.

Many insects look for a warm place in which to spend the winter. Ladybirds like cracks in walls, earwigs crawl under dead leaves and burrow into the soil. A layer of mulch offers a cosy winter blanket to many insects as well as protecting and enriching the soil.

You will often see people burning piles of garden waste in autumn. It would be much better for all the insects and other animals if these piles of twigs, branches and cut-off stalks were left over

the winter. Sometimes hedgehogs are burned alive if they have already made a home in such a pile. And it would be better for the garden if this garden waste was shredded in a shredder and spread over the soil. Talk with your parents and see if they will keep a heap of garden waste in a far corner of the garden, which will provide a winter home for hedgehogs and other animals.

Birds do not hibernate. Some migrate, or fly away, to warmer countries, but many stay here. They will find enough to eat as long as the ground is free of snow, and providing there are plenty of bushes with berries and grasses and flowers with seeds. Sunflowers offer birds a real feast!

If snow is covering the ground then the birds will be very grateful for a feeding station. Feeding stations need to be placed or designed so that the feed doesn't get wet, because wet feed rots and makes birds ill. Some feeding tables are designed like a silo, so that a bird has to pick out what it wants.

Birds have all sorts of preferences when it comes to feed. Some like seeds containing oil, such as sunflower, poppy, thistle, and alder seeds as well as apple, melon and pear pips, beech nuts, walnuts and hazelnuts. Tits, finches and siskins like seeds.

Other birds prefer soft feed. They need dried wild berries, unsulphured raisins and currants, small pieces of fruit and rolled oats. Blackbirds, robins, wrens and hedgesparrows will eat this. If you set up two feeding stations with different food then it is more likely that every bird will manage to get something to eat.

There is one more thing to think about in winter. If it doesn't rain or snow for a long time then you should water the garden, but only if the soil isn't frozen. Plants do need water in winter, but not as much as in summer.

83

Garden Design

Gardens are usually made up of more than just a vegetable patch. There are usually trees, shrubs and flowers, a lawn or a meadow. There might be a terrace or an arbour, a hedge, fences and maybe even a small pond. Working out where everything should go and what it should look like is called designing a garden, and garden designing is a profession in itself. Garden designers are usually employed only when very large gardens or parks are planned.

Gardens are often fenced in or surrounded by walls. A fence can be made of wire or wood, while walls are usually made of bricks. Some walls and fences can be rather ugly, and they can be hidden behind plants. Hedges are often used for this. They are usually made of evergreen plants and are cut regularly so that they keep an even shape. They can also be made of a variety of plants, which looks more interesting. You can use climbing plants to hide fences.

You could make a drawing of your garden like this. Your parents might help to remind you where everything is. You can probably work out what the arrow is pointing to: the children's plot and Sunny the sunflower.

Nasturtiums or Canary creepers are good plants for this because they both grow very quickly. Vetch and mallow will also cover a fence with pretty flowers and leaves.

Most gardens have at least one tree. A tree that is too big for a garden could cast a shadow over the house as well as the garden, so it is important to make sure that the size of the tree is appropriate to the size of the garden. In general small gardens require small trees. Nurseries sometimes sell small or dwarf varieties of trees that are naturally quite big. All deciduous trees lose their leaves in autumn, but before they fall they can turn brilliant red, orange, or yellow colours. Some trees have beautiful blossom in the spring. Pines, firs and other trees with needles instead of leaves have neither blossom nor coloured leaves, but they do stay green throughout the year, and that is why they are called evergreens.

Perennial plants are plants that live for more than one year. You should think carefully about where you plant them because they will live for many years. It is not a good idea to put them in a vegetable garden. Perhaps you could offer to look after one or two perennial plants in your parents' garden. Marguerite daisies and primroses are good perennials to start with.

Annual summer flowers can be planted wherever there is still room. You can plant different annuals each year, and then your garden will look different each year.

The lawn is usually in the middle of the garden. Lawns need a lot of care and attention. They need to be mown regularly and they may need watering in summer. If there is a terrace in your garden then you will probably find that your parents have planted fragrant flowers next to it so that you can enjoy their scent as you have dinner or read a book there. This is a good idea, but don't forget that it is not healthy to be out in the sun all day. A sun umbrella or an awning will protect you.

An arbour is like a little house formed by plants growing together. Sitting in a quiet arbour on a hot summer's day is one of the great pleasures of a garden.

A garden is made up of many different things, and can offer many different pleasures, from playing football on the lawn to reading under a tree to eating ice-cream on the terrace.

The Flower Garden

If you have planted vegetables in your garden then there won't be room for more than a few marigolds and tagetes, because vegetables need space to develop properly. Perhaps you could help your parents to look after their flowers. If you help them maybe they will let you pick a bunch of flowers once in a while. Flowers make a lovely gift to take to friends on their birthday, or to your grandmother.

The first flowers to appear in spring grow from bulbs. You are already familiar with hyacinths - remember, you read about how to force them indoors. Tulips, narcissi, snowdrops, bluebells, and daffodils all grow from bulbs. Some bulbs do not produce flowers until summer, like lilies, amaryllis and the various kinds of allium (alliums are flowers related to onions). Some spring flowers grow from corms, which look like a cross between a bulb and a root. These include crocuses, Winter Aconite and Dog Tooth Violets.

If you want these flowers in your garden for the spring then you will have to think ahead, as the bulbs, corms or tubers need to be planted in autumn, preferably in September or October. They like a loose well-drained soil

enriched with compost, and should be planted two or three times as deep as the bulbs or tubers are wide.

Most flowers bloom from May into autumn. Antirrhinums, or snapdragons as they are sometimes called, have interesting blooms. Seedlings are available from about May. They need to be spaced 12 centimetres apart. Snapdragons come in many different colours, and grow to 40 or 50 centimetres in height.

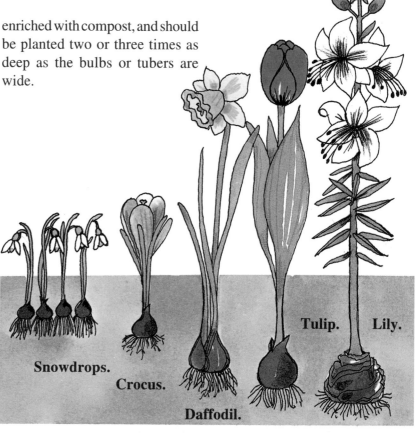

Snowdrops.

Crocus.

Daffodil.

Tulip.

Lily.

If you gently press the flower together from the side then it opens its 'mouth', which looks like a dragon's mouth. The mouth will 'snap' together again when you let go.

If you want to grow flowers for their fragrance then you can't do much better than mignonette. They may not look as pretty as roses or violets, but their fragrance is enough to knock you over.

Mignonette seedlings are available in spring, but they are easy to grow from seed. In this case you could sow them in small pots in April or sow them directly into the soil in May. Love-in-a-Mist has a flower pretty enough to match its name. It has delicate pastel flowers and very fine leaves which look like dill. Love-in-a-Mist can be sown directly into the soil in April.

Don't forget Sunny! There are various types of sunflowers, big as well as small. Why don't you try the really tall variety? It's fun to grow such a tall flower, even if you have to climb on a chair to look at it.

Gypsophila is another very pretty flower. Gypsophila flowers are those tiny white pompoms that grow on the end of fine, forked stems. Florists often add them to bunches of flowers. Sow gypsophila seed in May, about five centimetres apart. Try sowing a gypsophila seed between every other flower.

Have you ever seen and admired wild poppies and cornflowers? You can buy garden

You will get a lot of pleasure from a dwarf rose.

varieties of both these flowers. Iceland Poppies are an attractive variety.

Many types of flowers take more than a year to bloom. These are called biennials. This doesn't mean that they die after the second year, it just means that they take two years to grow. The seedlings spend their first year in nurseries and they are sold the following spring to you and other gardeners. Biennials include ox-eyed daisies, forget-me-nots, carnations, pansies, Canterbury Bells and many more.

Roses are often considered to be the queen of flowering plants. You have to be a bit careful around roses as most of them have sharp prickles. If you are interested in growing them then you might consider a dwarf rose. Dwarf roses grow to about 40 centimetres and are happy growing in pots and tubs on a balcony. They need plenty of sun and water and a rich, loose soil. Spread compost over the roots in autumn.

Dried Flowers

Flowers suitable for drying hold their shape and colour even when they are dry. There is one type of flower that doesn't change much at all when it is dry: the everlasting flower. They look like big daisies and are yellow, orange, red or white. Everlasting flower seeds can be sown in a sunny spot in the garden in mid-May.

Immortelles are similar to everlasting flowers. They are about the same size but their petals are narrower. They too like plenty of sun and should be sown in May.

If you want these plants to grow big and strong then each plant should be no closer than about 25 centimetres from its neighbour. Check the distance four weeks after sowing and thin them if necessary.

You can make lovely gifts for your friends from everlasting flowers and styrofoam balls.

Statice also dries well. Sow Statice seed in small pots indoors in early April. Plant out the seedlings in a sunny corner of the garden in late May.

Golden yarrow deserves a spot in your garden of everlasting flowers. Seedlings of this perennial are available in May.

One more plant should be included: Honesty. This is a biennial. Sow the seeds in July and thin the plants later to about 25 centimetres. They will bloom the following year in May. If this sounds too complicated, you could buy Honesty seedlings instead.

Drying flowers is not particularly difficult. the only slightly tricky part of the process is cutting the flowers at the right time. Let's start with Honesty,

which is different from all the other dried flowers, in that you want to dry the flat, oval-shaped seed pods that form after the plant has bloomed. Cut the stalks before the pods burst open, bind them together into a bunch and hang them upside down to dry - an attic or any other dry, airy place makes a suitable drying room. The brownish outside walls of the pod and the seeds should fall off, leaving the transparent, mother-of-pearl coloured inner wall. The plant takes its name from this transparent wall: it was thought that you could see into the soul of an honest person, just like you can see through the walls of Honesty.

Golden yarrow should be cut low down, bound together into a bunch and dried like Honesty. Cut Statice when the small blooms are at their fullest and dry it upside down. All other types of flowers should be cut before they are at their peak, then hung upside down to dry.

In a few weeks all moisture will have evaporated from the plants.

By now it will be autumn and you can probably find all sorts of other plants to include in your dried arrangements: the seedheads

Making a tree that blooms all year round.

of various grasses, twigs of coloured leaves or berries, and even bare twigs. You could ask your parents if you can clip a few twigs off an evergreen tree or shrub. It is often quite surprising how good some plants will look once they are combined with other things, even if they don't look very interesting on their own.

Dried flower and plant arrangements don't have to sit in vases. You could put them in a nice jug, a small basket or a clay flowerpot. Arranging the plants can be easier if you use florists' foam. This solid green foam is available from garden centres.

You cut off a piece of foam and squeeze it into the vase or pot (or whatever you're using) and then stick the ends of the plants into the foam.

Be adventurous with your arrangements! You could, for example, try making a tree. For that you need a flowerpot and some other things too. Stand a bamboo stick in the middle of the pot. Now half fill the pot with gravel. Next comes filler, which you can buy in hardware shops. This will hold the stick securely in place. If necessary, ask an adult to help you. Once the filler has dried you can carefully press a styrofoam ball down on to the stick. You will have to press the ball quite hard so that the stick pokes into the ball. Cover the ball with moss, which you can buy from florists or garden centres. Secure the moss with pins, and now you can decorate your tree with dried flowers, seedheads and whatever else takes your fancy. Poke the stems through the moss into the styrofoam ball. You might like to cover the filler in the pot too, since it doesn't look particularly nice.

Flowers hanging in bunches to dry.

89

The Garden Pond

A small pond is a great attraction in any garden. As long as you don't intend to keep fish the pond needn't be very big. If you want frogs to live there then the pond should be at least 80 centimetres deep at one point and preferably a bit deeper. Before you think about putting in a pond you should think carefully: do you feel confident in water? Could you get out if you fell in? If you have young brothers or sisters, or young children live next door and can get into your garden, then it would be safer to wait a few years.

There are plants that live in water and even underwater. Their leaves produce oxygen for the animals living underwater. Some plants, like waterlilies, float: their roots are in water but their leaves and flowers are above water. The water canna, which has small yellow flowers, is also a floating plant. Bog plants grow along the edges of the pond. Two very attractive examples are the marsh marigold and the blue water flag. Another group of plants likes to grow near water. They just enjoy the continuously damp soil and humidity that water creates. Globe flowers and rushes belong to this group of damp-loving plants, and many ferns appreciate a slightly shady spot near a pond.

A garden pond can become home for many plants and animals.

A pond will attract all sorts of animals, from the delicate dragonfly, with its transparent wings, to the mud snail, who ensures that the algae doesn't take over. The mud snail crawls over stones and scrapes the green algae off with its coarse tongue. There is a balance of nature in a pond, too. The water isopod eats dead and decaying bits of plants and prevents your pond from turning into a great smelly puddle full of rotting plants. Water spiders eat the water isopods and make sure that they don't take over the pond. Frogs in turn eat the water spiders when they come up to the surface to breathe.

You will have to help nature keep the balance in a small pond. You can do this by removing dead plants and thinning out those plants that seem to be taking over. Nature finds it difficult to do its job properly in very small areas. Ask your parents for help and advice.

Younger gardeners might need rather a lot of help to set up a pond. You can buy plastic pond liners at garden centres - these look like large tubs. A hole has to be dug to sink this liner into, and this is hard work, even for an adult! Bigger ponds are made with

Dragonfly.

Water skater.

a sort of plastic sheeting, but that is even more work.

Toads, frogs and other amphibians usually arrive at a pond as if by magic, but fish have to be introduced. Goldfish are the easiest and friendliest sort of fish to keep outside. Fish need water at least 80 centimetres deep. If the water is shallower than that, and you live in an area where there are severe frosts, it is safer to bring the fish indoors in winter. Otherwise they might freeze. Goldfish will mate and multiply if they feel at home. Keep a check on how many fish you have: there shouldn't be more than one fish for every cubic metre of water. Goldfish soon become quite friendly and will swim up as soon as you appear with a box of fish food. If you would prefer to have as natural a pond as possible you

should find out what sort of fish live in nearby lakes and ponds, and try to buy some of them. Ask your science teacher for advice.

No matter how small or large your pond, animals can drown in it. Many animals can swim, but just can't get enough grip on the slippery plastic sides to climb out, and become so exhausted they eventually drown. You can help them escape by keeping a plank in your pond. One end should rest on the bottom and the other end should reach right up to the ground at the edge of the pond. The animals can crawl or walk up the plank and escape from the pond.

A garden pond, together with its environment forms its own biotope. You can also introduce plants that are found in the wild. Some nurseries specialise in growing such plants.

Mini Ponds

You can set up a garden pond on a terrace or even on a balcony, using half a barrel, a pot or a bowl. Mini ponds like this are unfortunately too small for fish.

Making ponds in old barrels has become quite popular, so popular that you can buy them in garden centres. These barrels, which once contained whisky, herrings or pickles, have been cut in half, cleaned and are guaranteed to be watertight.

You can use any container as long as it isn't made of metal and is watertight. All sorts of old bowls and tubs can be used, and you can probably find something at home that will do. But be sure to check with your parents that you may borrow it.

As you can imagine a mini pond needs mini plants. These are not hard to find, and you can even get waterlilies in a miniature form, with flowers the size of a small coin. These dwarf waterlilies need water five to 20 centimetres deep.

Since mini ponds are usually on a terrace or balcony they are near people, and you can do everyone a favour by planting fragrant flowers in your mini pond, such as the Water Hawthorn. This needs at least 20 centimetres of water. Plants in a mini pond shouldn't be crowded. You can always make some mini-mini ponds (in a big yoghurt carton, for

example) and put them next to the bigger one. It is best to put them in the shade because the sun could warm up the small quantity of water in a mini-mini pond and start to cook your plants. Cypress grass would fit into a mini-mini pond. It usually grows indoors, but would enjoy spending summer outside in a pond. Cypress grass is a bog plant from the subtropics.

You could make a mini bog in another container and put it next to the pond. Bog plants such as marsh grasses and bulrushes always look attractive and are easy to grow. It is easy to make a mini bog. Plant the bulrush (or any bog

plant) in a pot with soil as you normally would. Now put this pot into another container, which must be watertight. Depending on the size of the pot, this could be something like a margarine tub or an old bowl. Pour water into the container so that it is a few centimetres deep. You could grow Cypress grass in a bog too. (Both bulrushes and Cypress grass will also grow in a pond.)

If there is any room at all left on your terrace or balcony you could place a fern alongside your mini ponds and bogs. Water plants do not need much in the way of nutrients and earth.

An old bath would make a good mini pond, as long as it is not all metal. Unfortunately it would be too small for fish.

You can make a good mini pond in a plastic flower box.

Let's say your pond container is 60 centimetres deep. Put in 20 centimetres of special fish-tank 'soil'. You can buy this at a garden centre or pet shop. Plant your waterplants and spread small pebbles over the soil to a depth of two centimetres. It is better to buy these pebbles from a garden shop as well. Now you add the water. The water should be lime-free, and should be poured in slowly and carefully. Make sure that your mini pond is sitting where you want it to be before you add any water! Even a small mini pond is very heavy and difficult to move.

A mini pond doesn't need much attention. Top up the water occasionally with more lime-free water, and remove dead leaves and wilted flowers. Dead plant material starts to rot quickly if left in water.

You could make a water garden in a container for your windowsill. To do that you need a square or rectangular glass or plastic container. Pet shops sell water plants, sand and gravel for aquariums, and you can use them to make a water garden. The sand goes in first, then you plant the plants, then you decorate the surface of the sand with pretty stones or shells. Now for the tricky part: pour in the water, very slowly, very carefully. The water should be lime-free and at room temperature. And there you have it! A mini pond! In an aquarium fish provide fertiliser for the plants, and since you have no fish you will have to add fertiliser to the water. You can buy this fertiliser at a pet shop.

Plants you might like to have in your water garden include water milfoil, various types of water weed, water plantain, crypto-coryne and many others. Ask the assistants in the pet shop which plants would be suitable for the container you are going to use and the place you will keep it.

Cypress grass.

Dwarf waterlilies.

Aponogetonaceae.

List of gardening terms